Other books by Kyell Gold:

The Argaea Series:
Volle
The Prisoner's Release and Other Stories
Pendant of Fortune
Shadow of the Father
Weasel Presents

Dev and Lee:
Out of Position
Isolation Play
Divisions
(Book 4 coming July 2014)

Dangerous Spirits:
Green Fairy
Red Devil
Black Angel (2015)

Other books:
Waterways
In the Doghouse of Justice
The Silver Circle

Other Cupcakes:
Bridges, by Kyell Gold
The Peculiar Quandary of Simon Canopus Artyle, by Kevin Frane
Science Friction, by Kyell Gold
Dangerous Jade, by Malcolm Cross
Winter Games, by Kyell Gold
Indigo Rain by Watts Martin

THE MYSTERIOUS AFFAIR OF GILES

by Kyell Gold

THE MYSTERIOUS AFFAIR OF GILES

Published by FurPlanet
Dallas, Texas
http://www.furplanet.com

ISBN 978-1-61450-168-8
Printed in the United States of America
First trade paperback edition: February 2014

Cover art and interior illustrations by Sara Miles

To Dame Agatha
for all the inspiration

Acknowledgments

Many thanks to Huskyteer for "Brit-picking" the manuscript. Inauthentic-sounding words and turns of phrase were likely added in final edits after she last looked through it.

The setting: Tremontaine, a large manor house in England, 1951.

The servants of Tremontaine:

 Ellie Stone: Assistant cook, weasel.

 Miss Turner: Head cook, weasel.

 Flora Hayma: Housemaid, Asian otter.

 Abby Rose: Housemaid, white rabbit.

 Miss Kitt: Senior housemaid, roe deer.

Mr Pearson: Butler, Indian brown rat.

Donald: Valet, dhole.

The family and guest of Tremontaine:

 Mr Giles St. Clair: Head of the household, red fox.

 Mrs Kate St. Clair: Giles's wife, red fox.

 Miss Mary St. Clair: Their daughter, 24, red fox.

 Mr John St. Clair: Their son, 20, recently returned from America, red fox.

 Mr Martin Trevayn: Giles St. Clair's business partner in the company White Rose, stoat.

THE MYSTERIOUS AFFAIR OF GILES

Ellie had just put the mushrooms into the big copper pot and turned on the gas when the house telephone rang.

"I'm not changing dinner now," snapped Miss Turner. "And we can't do any serving, not with Mr Trevayn here." Like Ellie, the head cook was a weasel, with rather more grey fur on her short, sharp muzzle, and the generous waistline common to successful cooks that Ellie was still cultivating. She ripped the last clump of feathers from a chicken with savage joy and placed the carcass on the roasting pan with the others. "You answer the telephone and tell them that."

Ellie had already wiped her paws and hurried over to the phone. She did not think it was Mr or Mrs St. Clair, and she was correct. "Oh, Ellie," Abby's voice half-sobbed as soon as she picked up. "Please come up. I need you."

"I'll come as soon as I can," Ellie said, and replaced the receiver.

She turned to find Miss Turner's bright eyes on her, waiting for her to ask permission, so Ellie ran through her remaining obligations to dinner. With the mushrooms simmering, the only remaining task before the cooking started in earnest was the bread, which would need to be punched down again soon. But the mushrooms also needed to be stirred. "If I call Flora down to attend to the soup, Miss Turner, might I...?"

"Oh, go on with you," Miss Turner said. Grey her muzzle might be, but she'd lost not a bit of sharpness. "Whatever you youngsters get up to, you'd best be getting up to it before you're too old to enjoy it."

"You're not old," Ellie said gratefully, taking off her apron.

"You learn to enjoy different things at my age." Miss Turner pulled the last of the chickens toward her. "You be back here in forty minutes. And use the back stairs."

"I know, I know. Mr Trevayn." Ellie hurried to the door. "Thank you, ma'am. I'll be back."

She found Flora Hayma polishing the silver in the dining room and dispatched the small-clawed otter to the kitchen. "Bless you," Flora said, dropping the cloth in the drawer and slamming it shut with satisfaction. "Polishing is so *boring*."

Ellie took the stairs up to the servants' chambers two at a time. At the second floor landing, halfway up, the weasel paused and glanced out of the window, where a fox in a wide-brimmed sun hat and plain blue dress knelt by a row of flowers, bushy tail flowing out behind her. It wasn't until Ellie was halfway up to the third floor that she thought, *Now, that's odd…*

But at the door of the little room she shared with Abigail, all those thoughts fled from her mind. The pure white rabbit sat on the edge of her narrow bed, a robe held around her middle, her long black-tipped ears flopped back behind her head, but before Ellie had gotten the door closed behind her, Abby sprang to her feet and wrapped her arms around Ellie.

"Oh, Ellie, thank you! I'm so sorry, but I didn't expect—he just came in and said he needed me, and—well, I've just been sitting there feeling awful, simply awful—it was so quick—"

"Steady." Ellie kissed Abigail's nose and pushed the door closed behind them. It wouldn't lock, but Ellie didn't much care about that. Nobody but Flora was likely to come up here anyway, and Flora wouldn't leave the mushrooms, not under Miss Turner's eye. So Ellie slid her arms inside the robe and rubbed her paws through Abby's soft white fur, held her curves, and said, "Now, what happened? It was him?"

"I was cleaning the sink, and then he was there, and he said, 'Now, Abby, I think that porcelain's quite clean enough.'" She trembled, saying the words.

Ellie pulled the rabbit close and kissed the corner of her mouth. "Just like that. But that was Mrs St. Clair in the garden I saw just now. Did she come back unexpected?"

"No." Slowly, Abby's shivering calmed. She rested her paws on Ellie's hips. "That's the thing. He watched her out the window the whole time he was on me. He didn't even look at me. Like he was enjoying that she was there. I warned him to lower his head, that she might see him. 'Let her,' he said."

"Good heavens." Ellie said the words in a soft, comforting tone while her paws worked a similar magic on Abby's fur. "That's different. Could you smell liquor on his breath?"

"No. It was *strange*." Abby took a breath. "And fast. Out and then in, and then…and then out again. And then gone, and he just said, 'Clean up, girl.' Not even a little kiss."

"I wonder if they've had a row." Ellie looked over Abby's shoulder at the window, which looked down onto the same garden.

"He's been like that for a month now. Not with Mrs Kate outside,

2

2

off

2

off

off

2

off

off

2

off

I mean, but—no kissing, or not much. I used to like being with him. It made him happy, you know, and he would smile and wag his tail after and tell me I'd made his day sparkle. Today I just feel like—like one of his appliances."

Ellie guided the rabbit back to the bed. "Well, I'll make up for that." She kissed the rabbit on the other side of her mouth, and then on the end of her short muzzle, and then on the patch of black fur just over her left eye. "Just lie down and I'll make up for everything."

"I can still smell him on me," Abby murmured, lying back obediently.

"Don't think of him." Ellie spread the robe wide and admired the slender beauty before her. It was no wonder Mr St. Clair wanted her. The wonder was that more people didn't. Lucky weasel, Ellie told herself.

Abby raised her head quickly, looking down her bare body at Ellie. "Did anyone see you come up? What if Flora...?"

"Flora's stirring soup in the kitchen, and anyway, she knows." Ellie quashed her irritation; after all, Abby needed her, and where else was one so soft and gentle to turn to be treated gently, in this hard world? She focused on enjoying the sight and feel of Abby's stomach, running claws below the line of the ribcage and down to the hipbones. "I suppose he didn't care whether you enjoyed yourself."

The soft white fur rose and fell, slowing. "Not this time."

"Then I'll make up for that, too." Ellie lowered her muzzle to Abby's stomach, inhaling the rabbit's lovely natural scent, and yes, she could smell the sharp musk of the fox atop the scent, too. "Just you lie back and imagine we're in our little room above our restaurant. Outside is Church Street, and you can smell the flowers from the cart girls. We have—"

"And I'm the hostess." Abby's voice took on a dreamlike quality. "People come from miles around to sample your dinners."

"Mmm." Ellie traced the curves above with a gentle paw, while her muzzle occupied itself elsewhere.

"Aaa-aand," Abby sighed, "we have lovely china, a Royal Copenhagen set with the blue patterns. Some paintings on the walls by local artists, you know, country bridges and fields and beautiful things like that."

Ellie smiled and continued her attentions until Abby's breathing quickened. "And tables...with white cloths...oh, Ellie...how many tables will we have?"

"Mmm. One." Ellie licked slowly. "Two." And again.

It was a rather small restaurant, that afternoon.

•

A short while later, they held each other, Ellie still in her plain cook's dress, Abby with not a stitch of clothing. "Feel better?" the weasel asked.

Abby nodded against Ellie's shoulder. "I smell better, too."

"You smell like me."

"That's what I mean."

Into the quiet of the room came raised voices. Ellie peered toward the open window. "There's a row going on."

"Who could be having a row at this time on such a nice day?" Abby's eyes were half-closed.

Ellie prodded her. "Don't go to sleep. You've got to serve dinner." She sat up and craned her neck, looking out the window. Down in the garden, Mrs St. Clair stood facing a fox in a driver's cap and brown suit, his tail flicking back and forth. "It's the master and missus. Maybe she did see him, before."

"Bother dinner," Abby said, and reached a thick paw up to Ellie's side. "Bother old Trevayn."

Ellie did not move away from the rabbit's paw. Another few minutes wouldn't hurt. And watching the row below her, she felt like one of the detectives in her police novels. Perhaps later, it would be important that the St. Clairs had fought in the garden at…six thirty? Tea had been over for an hour when she came upstairs. Perhaps six forty-five.

"I just want to stay here," Abby sighed.

Ellie turned from the window. "So you feel better about…about this?"

Her claw trailed along Abby's long ear. The rabbit flicked it and smiled. "Maybe a little? It's still so strange. I mean, you always hear people talk about 'those queers' and you think it's just boys, and they're perfectly nice, but a little odd. And then you turn around one day and you find that your best friend is one, and then…well, then you're one too, and it's all just…" She stared up at the ceiling and then laughed, but her laugh was shaky. "Well, queer, I suppose."

Below them, in the garden, Mrs St. Clair turned away abruptly and strode toward the greenhouse. Her husband, his tail flicking more agitatedly, took two steps after her and then stopped, shoulders slumped. "Should we be more like the master and missus?" Ellie mused. "Running behind each others' backs?"

"Oh, they love each other," Abby said. "But El, what do you suppose they *do* with each other?"

"What?" Ellie turned her sharp muzzle down, whiskers twitching in amusement. "I suppose what he just did with you, only possibly with more kissing."

"No, no." Abby swatted at her, sitting up. "And don't remind me of that. I mean, boy queers. How do you think—I mean—"

"Oh, boys are easy," Ellie said. She circled Abby's shoulders with an arm. "I can't stand that he abuses you like that. If we could be assured of finding another position together, we'd quit."

"It was a little nice at first," Abby leaned into Ellie. "If I didn't think about what it meant to Mrs St. Clair."

"How can you say he loves her when he does that to her?"

Abby was lost in her own world again. "I feel like an old shoe now. I expect he'll find someone else soon enough. Maybe he'll keep me on, like Miss Kitt."

"You're not an old shoe. You're an old soul, if anything." She kissed Ellie's ear. "You'll have me when he leaves you, not like poor old Kitt."

"I'm lucky." Abby's eyes met Ellie's, followed quickly by her lips.

•

Flora was polishing a spoon in the dining room when Ellie came down. "Did Miss Turner take over the soup?" Ellie asked.

The small-clawed otter looked up with a start. "No? Oh dear." She dropped the spoon she was holding. "You meant to *keep* stirring, didn't you?"

Ellie hurried into the kitchen, lifting her nose. She didn't smell anything burning, so she approached the big soup pot hopefully. But the ladle dragged along the bottom, and brought up a thick sludge of cream. She sighed and applied herself vigorously to the stirring, trying to scrape it off and dissolve it back into the warm soup.

At the entrance to the kitchen, Flora fidgeted with her paws. "I'm so sorry. I was stirring it, and I thought it seemed to be well-mixed, and I've never made soup before…"

"What's happened with the soup?" Miss Turner bustled back into the kitchen, both large paws holding bunches of greens from the garden. She threw them into the sink. "You've not let it burn?" Her nose twitched, and she took the ladle from Ellie.

"No," Ellie said, but Miss Turner's lips dropped into a disapproving frown as she dragged the ladle through the bottom of the soup.

"Well," she said. "If you apply yourself, it might be salvageable." She handed the ladle back and gestured to Flora. "And here, you can wash greens, can you not?"

"Oh, yes'm," Flora said.

"Then come and attend to these. Because Donald must clean the main rooms, I must go down to the village for the bread."

"I can go," Ellie said, just to offer, although she knew that stirring the soup was a punishment.

Miss Turner laughed. "I'm certain you could. But unless you'd like to bring that stove and soup with you, you'll stay here and stir it back to its proper consistency." With that, she swept out.

Flora ran the water, and didn't speak for the better part of two minutes. "I'm so sorry," she said finally.

"It's all right." Ellie stirred. The soup was beginning to loosen up. It would be fine in a little while.

"Look," the otter said. "If you like, I'll do the washing-up tonight."

"You don't need to do that. It was an honest mistake."

"No, I feel so terrible. Please let me." She paused. "Then you and Abby can spend the evening together, after she does Mr Trevayn's room."

"Bother him," Ellie said with nearly as much heat as was being applied to the soup. "I'm certain he hired a fox valet simply to annoy the master."

"It can't annoy the master much if Mr Trevayn never brings him to Tremontaine," Flora said. "He almost never visits anyway. What would be the point? I'm sure he hired the valet because he was an excellent valet."

"It's transference," Ellie said. "When he orders the valet around, he pretends it's Mr St. Clair, I'll wager."

"Oh, you with your psychology." Flora laughed. "If he wanted to annoy the master so much, he'd refuse to agree to sell White Rose."

"He hasn't the means to refuse anything. Mr St. Clair owns most of it."

"Mrs St. Clair doesn't want to sell." Flora nodded sagely when Ellie turned. The otter was standing with dripping paws held up in the air, half the vegetables washed and piled on the sideboard, half still floating the sink. "She's been very cold about it since Mister Trevayn arrived, and this morning at lunch she snapped at Mr Giles."

"They were having a row in the garden just now," Ellie said. "I wonder if that's what it was about. I don't know why Trevayn had to come here at all. Can't they arrange this in their office?"

"It was Miss Mary's idea, if you can believe that. She said she wanted to see more of what her father's business is about. And then with Master John coming back unexpectedly, it just made sense. Mr Giles will want him to join the family business, although if you ask me, Miss Mary is more likely to." She wiped her paws on her dress. "Not that she'll have a chance if they sell it. Maybe that's why Mrs Kate didn't want him to. They're having drinks in the parlour right now. I'll go in and see if the master and missus are still having their row."

She was in the doorway before Ellie called out. "Flora! Finish the greens, please?"

The otter returned to the sink with an abashed look. "Sorry, Ellie."

"If you really are going to do the washing-up tonight," Ellie said, "I'll lay the fires in the morning."

"Oh, you needn't do that! I'm helping out to make up for the soup." The otter's paws splashed through the water.

"I have to get up to do breakfast anyway," Ellie said, thinking to herself that Miss Turner washed vegetables with a good deal less sound and fury. "It's only half an hour earlier. And then you could sleep in 'til serving-time."

"Well..." Flora wavered. "If you're sure..."

Ellie was. The housemaid and assistant cook clasped paws to seal the bargain, and then Flora passed Ellie the towel, as she had forgotten to wipe her paws.

•

Dinner was normally a sedate affair. Ellie often managed it on her own, though Miss Turner remained in the kitchen watching and "making conversation"—which is how she described the passing on of things she'd heard about the house and from the various tradesfolk who brought supplies.

Tonight, however, Ellie and Miss Turner were kept busy, first ladling the mushroom soup into bowls, then tending to the small salads, while giving the oven a wide berth so as not to damage the gently rising soufflé. Abby ran back and forth from the dining room to the kitchen with orders and news; Donald, the other servant, and Mr Pearson, the butler, remained in the dining room.

"Miss Mary wants cheese with the soup," the rabbit said, hurrying back. "Have we got any?"

"Cheese?" Miss Turner lifted her head from glazing the chickens, and pointed at the large pantry. "Third shelf. What kind of cheese does she want?"

"She just said 'cheese.'" Abby brushed by Ellie on her way across the large kitchen. "What kind would be suitable?"

"Something with a bit of a tooth to it for Miss Mary, I'd wager," Ellie said. "She loves her Italian cheeses."

"We haven't got any Eye-talian cheeses just now." Miss Turner slapped the steaming carcass of the chicken, spreading the honey-wine scent of the glaze across the kitchen through the sweet aroma of the soufflé. "There's a cheddar there, try that. It's the block with a bit cut out of it. No, girl, don't just take the whole thing. Oh, Ellie, help her."

Ellie, grinning, pulled the block of cheese from Abby's fingers, letting her fingers brush the rabbit's. "Let's cut off a bit and grate it."

"How are they all getting on?" Miss Turner asked. "Has Master John come down from his nap?"

"He keeps yawning," Abby said, watching as Ellie deftly sliced a piece of cheddar cheese and then applied the grater to it. "He says when he woke up it was two in the morning in America and he should be asleep. How could it be two in the morning there when we're all waking here?"

"Because it's far away." Ellie kept her claws and fingers clear of the grater, and soon had a good pile of grated cheese. "The sun rises here before it does there. So it can't be half-six in the morning there when it is here. They'd be sitting about trying to have breakfast in the pitch dark."

"Or they'd be having supper at noon or some such nonsense," Miss Turner put in. "It's rum, him coming back right when he did. School's still in session even in America, I'd have thought."

"Maybe their schools close earlier," Abby said brightly. "On account of they're so far away."

Ellie kissed the rabbit on the nose. "You're a dear," she said. "Go and take this to Miss Mary, and there's enough there for the others if they want some. I'll put the cheese back."

Miss Turner watched Abby patter out of the kitchen and began carving the first chicken, the glaze on it having set. "That girl will trip over her little cotton-tail one day."

"Oh, Miss Turner," Ellie said. "Abby doesn't know much science, but she's got a good heart."

"Good heart and good nature get you taken advantage of in this world," the older weasel said. She brandished the knife. "Mark my words. But as long as she's got you looking out for her, I suppose she'll be all right."

"I will, as best I can," Ellie said.

"Speaking of," Miss Turner said, although it wasn't clear what she thought they'd been speaking of, for she went on immediately to talk about how John should've taken a boat to allow himself to adjust to the time change, and how it was just a matter of time before some immense disaster overcame a passenger airliner.

"Still," Ellie said. "The missus said Master John's flight took only fourteen hours. It used to take days to go to New York."

"People rushing about in a hurry." Miss Turner arranged the chicken pieces on a platter. "Oh, speaking of, who do you suppose ran up to me in the town to ask where Mister Giles has been?"

Ellie looked up and saw the other weasel's eye glinting. "I've no idea," she said, because Miss Turner was waiting for her to say it.

"Hope Cooper."

"The wolf?"

"Yes, her. And when she'd gone, Mister Bones said he'd seen Giles walking about with her. Nothing to cause a scandal, mind, if only it weren't Giles. People know what he gets up to."

The older weasel said it as though she were not one of the primary instruments of the spread of this information. "Hope Cooper," Ellie said. "Well, I never."

She finished the salads just as Abby came back in, followed by Donald, both holding large circular trays. "Help me with this," Miss Turner said, so Ellie hurried over to help loading up the trays as the rabbit and dhole held them steady. They placed the large platter of chicken in the centre of Donald's tray, and covered it with a silver bell, and then loaded Abby's tray with the sauce, the limp cooked French beans, the creamed potatoes, and the celery relish.

"See you at the salad course," Ellie whispered into Abby's long ear as the rabbit turned to go. The ear twitched; Abby smiled, and disappeared.

Miss Turner examined the soufflé. "Nearly done," she said, and then cast a bright eye over Ellie's salads. "Lovely. That one with the cucumbers is for Miss Mary?"

Ellie nodded. "She likes them."

"Good." The older weasel nodded and swung her short tail from side to side. "She's in good spirits anyway. Possibly the only one of the lot."

"Mister Giles seemed rather pleased."

Ellie thought she'd kept most of the bitterness out of her voice, but Miss Turner looked sharply in her direction. "He and Mrs Kate had a row in the garden."

"Oh, is that why you went out to collect the greens?" Ellie controlled her grin.

The older weasel swatted her just beside the tail. "Mind your cheek, girl."

"Well, what was it about?"

Miss Turner huffed. "They stopped before I could hear. I wager it was about that Trevayn. Mrs Kate doesn't like him." She paused. "Or maybe Mrs Kate heard about one of Mister Giles' little trips to the village."

Talking about Giles' affairs brought back memories of Abby sitting hunched on the edge of the bed. Ellie grasped at the only other subject she could think of, the discussion with Flora foremost in her mind. "I think it was about White Rose. Mrs Kate doesn't want them to sell it."

"Well, of course she doesn't." Miss Turner dusted her paws on her apron and bent to look at the soufflé again. "Not as though she has any say in it. Let's take that out. Careful, now, or it'll fall."

They lifted the heavy casserole dish together and gently placed it on the sideboard just as a large, slender roe deer in a proper black dress with immaculate white trim entered the kitchen from the back way. "I'm just fetching the tea for Mrs Kate's rooms," she said, going right to the pantry.

"Careful of the door!" Miss Turner hurried to the door the deer had let swing behind her, catching it before it slammed shut.

"Mrs Kitt, look at our lovely soufflé," Ellie said.

The deer paused and fixed the soufflé with such a baleful eye that Ellie thought it might fall from that alone. But it stayed bravely up, and the deer turned back to the cupboard. "Extravagance. You haven't moved the tea, have you, Marjorie?"

Miss Turner rolled her eyes for Ellie's benefit. "Of course not, Eunice."

"Oh," Ellie said, moving to the cupboard. "Flora was in here serving tea…"

The roe deer let out an impressive sigh that ruffled the wax paper in the pantry. "It could be anywhere, then."

"There's Orange Pekoe here." Ellie had hoped to find the appropriate tea quickly, sparing Flora the wrath of Miss Kitt, but the distinctive tins were nowhere to be seen. She looked around the kitchen.

"She will definitely need the Earl Grey tonight," Mrs Kitt said. "With the house so full. I will have a talk with Miss Hayma about putting things back in their proper place."

The strong taste of the Earl Grey masked Mrs St. Clair's sleeping powder. Ellie tried to remember where Flora had put things. "Oh, here it is," she said. "In the refrigerator beside the milk."

Mrs Kitt stepped back from the open door of the refrigerator, nostrils flared. Ellie reached in and took the small wooden box, then closed the door quickly. She didn't mind the White Rose contraption, and in fact rather liked the chill it gave milk and butter. The older servants would have nothing to do with it, and even Miss Turner used it begrudgingly; Ellie often found the butter in the larder.

With the refrigerator door closed, Miss Kitt relaxed and shook her head as she took the box from Ellie by her fingertips. "I only hope the flavour of the tea is not affected by the chill." With that, she swept out of the room.

"If it were," Miss Turner murmured to Ellie, "she'd be affecting it far more than the poor old refrigerator."

Ellie giggled, and Miss Turner went on. "Extravagant indeed! The war's been over six years, but she would still have us rationing cheese and butter."

Before Ellie could point out that her family still did not have the cheese and butter that the St. Clair household did, Abby came back in for the salads. "Oh," she said, "that soufflé don't look half majestic. If that don't cheer up the table, nothing will."

"How did they like the chicken?" Miss Turner asked.

Abby tilted her head so that the tip of one ear flopped to the side. "Mrs Kate said it was lovely. Miss Mary said the glaze tickled her nose."

"It's made to do that for fox noses." Miss Turner looked pleased.

"And Mr Trevayn said it was very safe."

"Safe?" Miss Turner raised a paw as if to strike the sideboard, and then her eye fell on the soufflé and she let her paw fall gently to her side. "Safe? What the devil does he mean by that? Safe?"

"I'm sure I don't know, ma'am." Abby held her tray out to Ellie, who began to pile salads on it. "But Mr Giles, he said, 'It's still good, isn't it, Trevayn?' and then Mr Trevayn allowed as how it was good."

"Safe." Miss Turner's eyes glowed. "I'll give him 'safe.' Donald!" The dhole had just entered the kitchen, and now looked startled at being addressed so immediately. "Does Mr Enfield have that foreign chilli sauce in his store at present?"

Donald stammered. "Ma'am, I have, I have not been to Mr Enfield's store, not in many days, and, and—"

"Well, go down in the morning and bring back some of that chilli sauce you and Flora had me put on your supper last month."

"In the morning, ma'am, yes, I can do that."

"Good." She rubbed her paws together. "I'll give him 'safe.' Little London snob, he is."

"I'm sure he didn't mean it that way," Abby murmured.

Miss Turner ignored her, her attention fixed on the dhole. "What did you come back for?"

"Oh," Donald said, "Miss Mary would like a little extra honey for her chicken and her vegetables."

"The dear," Miss Turner said. "Ellie—"

But Ellie was already moving to the pantry. "I'll fetch it."

"And," the dhole went on, "Master John, he asked for a, for a tomato sauce with his potatoes."

"Tomato sauce?"

"Yes. He said in America they put tomato sauce on most everything."

"On creamed potatoes?"

Donald looked away from the piercing gaze. "Miss Turner, ma'am, I am sure I do not know."

"Tch!" She turned, but Ellie had already brought a can of tomato sauce from the cupboard. "I suppose they have tomatoes in America at any time of year. He can have the emergency can. Donald, buy another one tomorrow when you go into the village."

"Ma'am, yes, I will." The dhole looked relieved. His ears came up and he even smiled.

"Speaking of," Miss Turner said, and lowered her voice, "are they all getting along in there? It's been terribly quiet."

"Mrs Kate seems quite cheerful," Abby said. "She talked about the flowers and how lovely the garden's coming along. She asked if they might hire some help for Mr Trundle, and Mr Giles said yes without a thought. And then Mr Trevayn said that help was expensive and Mrs Kate got very cool and laid her ears back and said they can afford it."

"She doesn't like him," Miss Turner observed. "And I should think the feeling's quite mutual."

"Oh, Mr Trevayn's all right," Ellie said. "Just because we've got to stay out of sight while he's around."

"I don't mind that," the cook said. "It's right and proper. I wouldn't want his valet here either. But there's just something about him. He seems to be, well, nasty sometimes."

"I don't think he meant it to be nasty," Abby said. " 'Safe' can be a good thing too. I'd quite like to be told I was safe."

She exchanged smiles with Ellie, while Miss Turner threw up her paws. "That's not what I mean. Now you've got your salads and your honey and," as Ellie put a small bowl of tomato sauce on Donald's tray, "your American tomato sauce. Go on back with you before Mr Pearson comes in and scolds me for keeping you."

Abby and Donald hurried out. Ellie smiled at Miss Turner as they prepared the serving-dish for the soufflé. "You won't really put chilli sauce in Mr Trevayn's food, will you?"

"I'd do more than that to someone who's insulted my food," Miss Turner said. "You just try me."

•

Ellie's last job of the night was to put together the servants' supper. There was quite a lot of chicken left over, and the soup was easily heated again on the stove. The French beans had been very popular, and not much was left of them, but for most of the servants, chicken with mushroom soup, creamed potatoes, and some crusts of bread was more than adequate.

They crowded around the small table in the kitchen, which was half the size of the master dining room table where five had recently supped, but was quite spacious enough for two cooks, two housemaids, a senior housemaid, a footman, a valet, and a butler.

The conversation flew smartly, led by Miss Turner and Flora, who sat at opposite ends of the table. Portly weasel and skinny otter shared their observations about the disposition of Mr Trevayn, the return of the younger St. Clair cub from America, the excitement of the older St. Clair cub at the White Rose business meetings, and, most especially, the state of the marriage of Mr Giles and Mrs Kate St. Clair.

This topic dominated many a servants' supper, more so when Eunice Kitt was not present. Tonight, even though the roe deer made several "Tut" noises, Marjorie Turner's new information about the village girl Hope having been seen with Mr St. Clair dominated the conversation.

"It needn't mean anything even if he is walking about with her," Miss Kitt said, with a steely look at Miss Turner. "People will gossip."

"Oh, that they will," the weasel agreed cheerfully. "Three different people told me they'd seen him walking with her. And it's often at times when her mother is away from the house, when they might be in there undisturbed."

"Idle speculation and jealousy," Miss Kitt sniffed. "How do they even know it's he?"

The rest of the conversations had died; the heads turned back and forth between deer and weasel as the two volleyed. Miss Turner did not disappoint. "Recognised his family crest on the tie, there you are."

"Master John wears the same tie," the roe deer parried.

"Oh, pshaw." The weasel speared a piece of chicken on her fork and bit it savagely. "Master John hasn't left this house for more than an hour since he returned, and anyway, two of the times were before that."

"Master John did come back early from America." This was Flora, taking back her role in the conversation. "I'll lay you two to one he got a girl in trouble."

"There's to be no wagering in the staff," Mr Pearson said, and then returned his attention to his soup.

"Don't be ridiculous," Miss Turner scoffed. "We'd have heard about it. Anyway, why would he have to leave the country?"

"Not the country, just the school."

"He would've told his father. That's something Giles'd be proud of."

"Maybe he did. He was only here a day before Mr Trevayn arrived, and Mister Giles has been so distracted."

"Oh, that Mr Trevayn."

There followed a general round of agreement on the character of the stoat, even from the reticent butler.

"He said of Tremontaine that it was 'so quaint to keep the original moulding.'"

"He keeps calling Donald to polish his shoes or press his shirts."

"It's because he leaves that valet of his at home."

"Well, he has to, doesn't he?"

"Whyever would he hire on a fox as his valet?"

"Ellie reckons it's because he resents Mister Giles bossing him around in the company."

That was Flora, again. Ellie glared at her, while the rest of the table stared at Ellie. "It's just a thought," she said.

"He was snooping."

Ellie was grateful that Miss Kitt took everyone's attention with that statement. The roe deer lifted her head and returned the gazes coolly. "Around where?" Flora breathed.

"The second floor. Outside the master's study this afternoon. I believe the master was locked in writing letters."

"Locked in?" Miss Turner rubbed at her whiskers, but Ellie only saw that out of the corner of her eye, because she was staring at Abby.

"He pretended he'd dropped something when he scented me. But I know what he'd been doing." She looked archly around the table.

Ellie knew, too, and moreover, she knew what he'd seen. Abby hadn't put two and two together yet, it looked like. "Well," the weasel said, getting up, "I'm setting the fires for Flora in the morning, so I'll be off to bed."

"Oh." Abby looked down at her empty plate and didn't say anything.

"I'll be up after I've done the washing." Flora smiled brightly at the two of them.

Ellie had no illusions that her relationship with Abby was a secret from the more sharp-eyed and keen-nosed staff. You couldn't live in close quarters with a pair of lovers and not realise it, not if you really kept an eye out. But the nice thing about being in a relationship with another female was that the people who admitted such a thing was possible and would therefore notice it were also generally the people who didn't mind it. The ones who objected to it, called it unnatural and perverted, those were the ones who wouldn't suspect even if Ellie kissed Abby right in front of them.

But Abby was still too nervous to do something as forward as walk up to bed with Ellie, even though Flora did it all the time. It was something Ellie knew would take time.

So she walked out, down the dim servants' hallway, and then paused near the entrance to the drawing-room. The servants' door had been left ajar, as it often was; the servants sometimes lingered at this point in the dim back hallway to listen to conversations. Indeed, as Ellie paused, words came clearly to her. "I should never have come back," a young male voice said.

Master John had left in Ellie's first year of service, and she'd barely known the moody, withdrawn cub of seventeen. Now, three years later, she only placed his voice out of process of elimination: it was too quick and deep to be the elder Mr St. Clair, and it wasn't nasal enough to be Trevayn. A moment later, she caught the scent of fox—more than one.

"You're imagining things." His sister's voice could almost have been their mother's, for it had that same sharp rhythm, but there was a softness in Miss Mary's voice that her mother had grown out of, if she'd had it at all.

"He said he was going to cut me off," John said. "No more college, no more travel. He said I could start as a clerk in White Rose. A *clerk*!"

"He means well. He wants you to be—"

"He wants me to be Giles St. Clair, Junior. He might as well have named me that."

"John…"

"It's easy for you," John said. "Daddy's little girl."

Mary laughed. "Oh, I have my secrets. Worse than yours, I daresay. But I have the good sense not to get thrown out of college for them."

"No…" John's voice slowed. "He won't let you even go to college."

There was silence, during which Ellie started to move back down the hall. But as she passed the door, she couldn't help looking through it. John stood with his paws pushed into his pockets, his bushy tail curled down, his ears flat. Mary faced him, ears upright, but her eyes were distant.

"No…" she said. "But that's about to change."

"Ha," John barked. "You think old Pater selling the company will make a difference? The only way things will change is if he's gone. Completely."

"Don't, John." But Mary's expression, to Ellie's eyes, was demure, her protest more rote than heartfelt.

"Oh, I know. He's strong as a prize-fighter. He's not dying anytime soon."

Ellie reflected that Master John had changed quite a bit. He was a little taller, she thought, had filled out his frame, and there was a little American edge in some of his words. Perhaps he'd gone out for sport in America as his father had always pushed him to do here.

"You sound as though you'd like him to."

"Well, it would make things easier, wouldn't it? For Mother, at least."

"Oh, John. They love each other."

"Ha." Again the bark. "You think so?"

"You've been away three years."

"So I have." John reached out and touched Mary on the shoulder. "I recommend it."

"Ellie!"

Abby said it, surprised, coming into the hallway from the kitchen. Ellie jumped away from the door, having just enough time to see both foxes' ears perk up before they were cut off from her view. She waved frantic paws at Abby, who widened her eyes and ducked through the door nearest her just as the drawing-room door opened.

"Ellie?" Mary looked curious. Behind her, John's brow and ears were lowered. His whiskers flicked up and back.

"Sorry, Miss St. Clair," Ellie said. "I was just going up to bed."

"But surely…" Mary looked up and down the hallway. "I heard your name being called?"

"How much were you eavesdropping on?" Now more than a hint of American edge roughened John's voice.

"John," Mary said reproachfully.

"I didn't hear anything!" Ellie cried, and grasped at the last thing she could remember. "Only something about your parents loving each other."

Mary looked down the narrow, poorly lit passageway again. The sun had gone nearly all the way down, and shadows crept up the walls and along the floor. "Well, they do love each other."

"Yes'm."

"Go on up to bed."

"Yes'm." Ellie curtsied. "Thank you, miss."

She hoped fervently that Abby would have the sense to come up another way, or at least to wait until the two foxes were well clear of the hall. John lifted his nose to the air, but Ellie was reasonably sure—as sure as she could be after four years living with a family of foxes—that the scents of the servants were equally thick in the back hallway, and even a young fox would not be able to pick out that Abby had stood twenty feet away for thirty seconds.

She didn't wait around to find out, but hurried along the hallway and up the back stairs to her quarters.

Properly, Ellie should have lived in the cook's quarters adjacent to the kitchen, while Abby shared one of the third floor rooms with Flora, and the senior housemaid, Miss Kitt, lived in the other. But Miss Kitt's rheumatism did not agree with stairs, so she had taken Ellie's bed on the first floor, and Flora had taken Miss Kitt's so that Abby and Ellie could be alone. True, Flora did not give much thought to which of the two doors she walked into when coming up to her chambers; she had lived in the room that was now Abby's for two years, and the habit was difficult to break.

For that reason, Ellie paused before taking off her dress. But Flora was downstairs doing the washing-up, and Ellie was tired and worn down. Having guests was bad enough, but all this homecoming, and Giles going after Abby in the afternoon with his wife in the garden, and then being caught snooping barely minutes after Miss Kitt had been condemning Mr Trevayn for the same thing…well, it was a lot for a poor weasel to handle, and Ellie was quite glad to see the tail end of this day.

Scarcely had she stretched out on the bed, without even the time to reach for one of the novels that stood on the small shelf at the bedside, when Abby burst through the door. "Oh, Ellie! I'm so sorry! I didn't know!"

"Don't be sorry," Ellie said, and then laughed softly as Abby fell on her, wrapping arms about her neck. "You'd no way of knowing, and anyway, I don't think there's any harm done."

"If I'd known you were listening at doors, I'd have been much quieter."

"Now, see here," Ellie said. "I wasn't—"

But she came up short, because of course that's exactly what she had been doing. Abby's wide blue eyes met hers. "Well. I suppose I was."

Abby's concern melted into a smile. She settled herself in the bed and rested her head on Ellie's chest. Her ears settled around the weasel's neck and she sighed. "Hear anything interesting?"

"Probably not," Ellie murmured. She reached up to stroke the back of Abby's head. "Master John isn't happy. And he *was* kicked out of the college. Miss Turner was right."

Abby closed her eyes. "Oh, good," she said. "She'll be so happy."

•

The sun had not yet come up when Ellie's alarm rattled her violently from her dreams. She reached out to quell the alarm, and Abby stirred beside her. "You don't have to get up yet," Ellie told her, sliding easily out of bed.

"I'm up," Abby murmured. "I'll help you with the fires."

Ellie watched as Abby yawned, closed her eyes again, and lay still. She smiled, got dressed, and went downstairs.

The sun was just glimmering over the horizon by the time she had the fires laid on the first floor. There were just the library and morning-room on the second floor to do.

Ellie walked up the grand staircase boldly. Mr Trevayn would not be awake yet, not until after sunrise, so there was no reason for her to stay hidden. And she loved the grand staircase, the beautiful marble steps and the smooth banister, the newels carved like fox tails and the portraits of the St. Clair family that hung on either side of it. The portraits were hidden in shadow with the stairway lights out, but she caught the faint scents of the preservative oils as she walked past, and they made her smile. She felt a part of history here, a part of a family line that had lived in Tremontaine since Richard II had deeded it to Bartholomew St. Clair for his valour in battle. Ellie's family lived in a crowded little shack on the outskirts of London, and though she was not a fox, she was much happier being a part of this family.

At the top of the staircase, she paused. The sunrise would be lovely, and there would be nobody out on the terrace overlooking the gardens. She could dally for a few moments. Nobody would catch her, and anyway, the fires in the library and morning-room wouldn't be lit until after breakfast. She had to start breakfast, too, but she had plenty of time for that. She strode out through the glass door for a well-earned rest.

The sunrise *was* lovely, rose-orange tendrils pushing a light pink glow into the early morning darkness. Below her, she could see glimmers of white roses and shadows of darker begonias, of chrysanthemums just starting to show their blooms and the pale white gravel path curving around the lily pond. The water of the pond reflected the sunrise back to her, and all in all, Ellie thought, this was one of those perfect moments one experienced from time to time.

She wished Abby were here with her. By the time she ran up and roused the rabbit, though, the sunrise would be brighter, and the delicate pastel hues gone. Likely there would be people about, and definitely birds—already a thrush was greeting the dawn, and another joined it as she listened. No, she would just have to tell Abby about it later.

Part of her hoped that Abby would have woken up and would be coming through the doors to join her. She turned, and in the space between birdsongs, she thought she heard motion from inside the house. And then a light male voice said, "Oh, there you are."

Guiltily, Ellie took a step toward the door, preparing excuses in her head—she'd heard a noise, had come outside to investigate—when something inside the house exploded.

The report made her flatten her ears. There was another sort of noise, but she couldn't register what it was, and then a moment later her brain sorted out what she'd heard.

A shot! Someone's fired a gun!

A creak came from the house, and Ellie didn't wait to hear what would happen next. She ran for the end of the terrace and the winding stone steps that led down to the garden.

At the bottom of the steps, her feet crunched on the gravel, and she hurried toward the pond, along the path that would take her around the side of the house and to the servants' entrance behind the kitchen, where the tradesfolk came. She had no other thought but to get into the house; in her mind, a shadowy figure with a gun was loping silently after her, just below the light of dawn.

Right as she drew level with the pond, she felt something pass in front of her face and strike the water with a loud splash. She squeaked and then clamped her paws over her muzzle and stopped dead. The pounding of her heart was the loudest thing for miles around.

A slow creak sounded from above, and now she knew what that sound was. One of the windows on the second floor was being slowly closed. Or opened.

Ellie found the grass verge of the path nearest the house. It was wet with dew, but she didn't care; it was silent and that was all that mattered. She hurried along it, rounded the corner of the house, and got to the side entrance. The door stuck; she bit her lip, cursing silently, and pulled harder on it. The shadowy figure in her mind was already creeping through the garden, gun at the ready. Her paws slipped from the handle, damp with morning dew, and she swallowed a sob, grabbing at it again.

This time the door came open easily, albeit with a small creak that sounded as loud as the gunshot to Ellie's ears. She hurried inside, closed it behind her, and leaned against the inside wall, panting.

Her police novels had never conveyed the sheer terror of being near a gunshot for the first time. Being in the war had been bad enough, but you were always on edge then, always half-expecting an explosion. The report shattering the peace of morning was worse, because here at Tremontaine she had not thought she would ever have to worry about that.

She heard many sets of footsteps in the house, and then someone screamed.

●

"Someone ought to call the police."

"Miss Kitt's doing that."

"Oh gracious God."

"It's all right, Mother."

"It must have been…a prowler?"

"The terrace door is open."

Ellie didn't say anything. She couldn't take her eyes from the sprawled body of Giles St. Clair, his tail hanging down onto the first step of the

grand staircase, head tilted to one side with the long russet muzzle slightly
agape and the eyes staring glassily. Death had caught him in the moment
of understanding, and he would never escape it.

His dark business suit lay open over a white shirt that had been clean
and pressed half an hour ago, and now bore a hole and wide red stain
in its centre. His tie lay haphazardly across his chest, curved as though
veering away from the stain and pointing down to where the fox's suit
jacket lay open on the right side.

Blood had soaked through the carpet and still dripped down onto
the first stair, a dark pool questing its way toward the limp white tail-tip.
Ellie, crouching on the next stair down while the rest of the household
crowded around the body, reached up to move the tail-tip away from the
blood.

Her paw was seized by another weasel's. "Don't move it," an imperious
voice said, and she looked up to see an older, stern stoat in a shirt and tie,
with dark pants. This must be Mr Trevayn.

In the flickering light of the oil lamp he carried in his other paw, his
fur looked a loam brown, with ivory under his muzzle, and his eyes were
an impenetrable black. "You're cold," he said.

Ellie wrenched her wrist away. "I've been up setting fires. And making
breakfast downstairs." Abruptly she realised that she was in the presence
of a guest of her own species, and she backed up so quickly she nearly fell.
"I'm sorry, I shouldn't be here."

"Quite right." Mr Pearson stepped down to join her. The large brown
rat's paw on her shoulder felt warm. "Go back to the kitchen. We will still
need breakfast."

Not all of us, Ellie thought, but she hurried down the stairs, casting
a glance back. Mrs St. Clair remained next to the body, sobbing quietly
on her knees while Mary knelt with an arm around her and John stared
down, ears flat, glaring at the body as though his father had died to offend
him. Mr Trevayn now had his back to her, talking quietly to Mr Pearson,
and Abby and Flora had been sent to their apartments.

As she reached the dining room, she heard Miss Kitt in the parlour.
"...Tremontaine. Yes, please send someone immediately. I'm afraid there's
been an accident."

An accident. How proper, how appropriate, how completely wrong.
Ellie's heart pounded as she made her way through the small pass-through
into the kitchen. She was the only one who'd witnessed the crime, but
what could she tell the police? Nothing of use. She hadn't seen the

She reached up to move the tail tip away from the blood.

murderer; hadn't even seen Mr Giles. She'd only heard him call out to her. And perhaps if she hadn't distracted him, he would have seen the murderer coming up on him, maybe he would have cried out the name, or been able to run down the stairs and away…

This was another thing her police novels could never have prepared her for, the flood of emotions on seeing her employer's body. He'd been terrible to Abby, and yesterday Ellie had hated him, but now all she could see when she pictured him was that expression of surprise, and she heard the shot again, and felt the terrible weight of having heard his last words and not having been able to give him any comfort in death. She took eggs from the pantry and butter from the refrigerator, but on the way to the sideboard, her paws began to shake, and she had to sit down on the floor with the breakfast in her lap. Her breathing came quick and fast, and then she brought her paws to her face and she cried.

•

Breakfast had been a quick, sombre affair. She'd boiled eggs and toasted bread, and Flora had served it efficiently. Abby was tending to Mrs St. Clair, who did not come down; only John, Mary, and Mr Trevayn took the breakfast.

Flora had tried to talk to Ellie, but Ellie just shook her off, and as a consequence, she heard Mr Trevayn clearly in the dining room telling the children that they needn't worry about money, that he was going to take care of the company as the now-senior partner. Ellie couldn't hear the children, but one of them must have asked about inheritance, because Mr Trevayn said, "You know, I honestly don't know whom your father's shares pass to. We'll have to look into that."

And the police had arrived in the middle of it and had advised everyone that they would be taking statements, and then when they saw that Mr St. Clair was dead of a gunshot wound, they had to call down to Sherbourne for an Inspector. Miss Kitt offered them breakfast, and so thankfully there was more cooking for Ellie to do. By this time, Miss Turner was up, but she busied herself finding out what had happened and saying, "How terrible!" over and over, and so it was Ellie who did most of the second breakfast service.

By half past ten, the house was in a state of thick tension. None of the staff were allowed to do any of their duties for fear of disturbing some piece of evidence, but neither did they want to stay in their quarters. So they gathered in the kitchen and in the back hallway, talking in hushed tones, while Mr Trevayn closed himself in the writing-room to make phone calls, and John and Mary sat with their mother in the parlour, and the police walked with clicks of their claws up and down the marble staircase.

Ellie and Flora sat with their paws clasped at the kitchen table, while outside they could hear Miss Kitt and Mr Pearson murmuring in the hallway. "When do you suppose they'll want to talk to us?" Flora asked. "I didn't see nothing. I was in bed. Did you see anything?"

"No," Ellie said. "Stop asking. In my novels, they usually just question people. But they're probably questioning the family first." In fact, she had tried to focus on how one of her police novels would go if this murder were at the centre of it, because it helped her distance herself from the emotions of having witnessed the crime, thinking about the gunshot she'd heard and imagining Mr Giles falling and dying while she ran down the stairs.

She rather thought she would have started by questioning the staff. Staff heard things that often the family didn't; for example, Abby and Ellie, and possibly Miss Kitt, would have testified about Mr St. Clair's philandering. Abby, who was Mrs St. Clair's personal maid when she needed one, could have testified to things like the sleeping-powder she took in her tea, while Mrs St. Clair's own husband might not have known that she took it, let alone how much.

Outside, the noise of conversation picked up. Ellie pricked her ears, but couldn't make out any of the words. And then Miss Turner came back into the kitchen, her eyes bright. "The inspector from Sherbourne's come," she said. "Name's Bennett. He's a big badger, and he says he wants to talk to all of us." She paused, dramatically. "Separately."

Before they could answer, she'd swept through the door and into the hallway. Over the sound of her repeating her proclamation, Ellie and Flora looked at each other.

"Well, I don't know what I'll be able to tell him," Flora said. "I was still in bed. Did you see anything?"

"I hope Abby's all right." Ellie had not seen the rabbit since before breakfast.

"She's taking care of Mrs Kate." The otter nodded her head. "Nothing keeps you occupied like looking after someone else who's worse off. I worked in a dispensary during the war, you know, when we couldn't get butter but every other day and a cake like you made last night, well, we could have one of those once a year."

"Soufflé," Ellie sniffed.

"God bless you. Oh, I see. Well, no, we made do all right. Bread with a little honey, that's sweet enough for a dessert, and we lived near a bee-keeper, so we would get honey. He was a dear old badger, but a little daft. Used to talk of the bees like they were people and the hives had personalities. 'This honey's from the scatter-brained hive,' he would say, 'so I can't vouch for the quality of it.' Of course it was all wonderful, you know, or at least we thought so. Better than sugar, although my mum always had a fondness for sugar. Her mother never used it growing up, of course. Out in India it's not quite so common, so we use other sweeteners, but mum said her first taste of sugar was like someone'd opened up a little piece of heaven. And to me it's so ordinary now." She sighed. "I suppose the point is…"

A policeman, a young wolf, poked his head into the kitchen. "Ladies," he said. "The Inspector would like a word with each of you."

•

"Your name, please, and your place on the staff."

The young wolf sitting next to the large badger had introduced himself as Sergeant Cooke. He spoke, pencil in one paw, notepad in the other, while the badger's eyes remained half-lidded. He appeared to be napping, but the wolf in his crisp police uniform watched Ellie closely. She swallowed. "Ellie—Elsinore Stone. I'm the assistant cook."

"And you've been at Tremontaine how long?"

"Four years. Four and a half, really."

"Thank you. Now, where were you when you heard the shot?"

"I was downstairs in the kitchen just getting breakfast started." Ellie had rehearsed this answer. In the hours since the murder, nobody had confessed to seeing her on the terrace, or seeing her come in the side door. If she said she'd seen the murder, she reasoned, then whoever'd done it would think she might've seen him, too. And then, if the police didn't catch him right away (they never did in the books she read), she would be the second victim. Granted, she was alone in the room with the two policemen, but policemen *always* let slip the wrong piece of information to the wrong person. Besides which, she had no good reason for being out on the terrace, next to the murder, which would mark her as a Suspicious Character.

"You heard the shot and…?"

"I'd just gotten the eggs out. I put them back and rushed upstairs."

"Immediately?"

No, of course not. Everyone else had beaten her to the body. They would know she hadn't been the first one there. "Well, no. I wasn't sure what I'd heard. Then I heard other people moving about and running, and so I rushed out too."

The wolf and badger looked at each other, and then the badger spoke for the first time. He had a deep, rumbling voice, and he talked slowly, lingering over each word. "How long would you say it was between the time you heard the shot and the time you 'rushed upstairs'?"

Ellie swallowed and tried to figure in her head how long it had taken her to run down the terrace steps, around the garden, into the kitchen. "I'm not sure. A few minutes perhaps?"

"Not exactly 'immediately,'" the Inspector said.

"Well, no." Ellie's mind cleared as she set herself to fixing the problem of what she'd said. "One doesn't want to appear stupid about such things. It was a strange sound, especially for that time of the morning. I thought—it reminded me a bit of a bomb falling. I was in London at the beginning of the war, until my mum sent me off to the country."

"That was your post before this one?"

She nodded, glad to not be talking about the murder anymore. "I cooked for Mrs Hansham until '47. And then Mrs Kate was at a luncheon I'd helped with and happened to mention she needed an assistant cook, and so I came to Tremontaine. Miss Turner was the head cook, but she says she'd like to retire in another six or seven years, and I hope to take over."

"I see." The badger turned back to the wolf, who'd been writing industriously, and nodded.

The wolf looked up at her. "Do you know anyone who would wish Mr St. Clair dead?"

Ellie sat up a little straighter. "No, indeed."

"Had he had any recent quarrels? Anyone speak up with a grudge against him?"

"Well…" Ellie hesitated. "He was quarrelling with Mrs St. Clair in the garden yesterday afternoon. I saw them from the window."

"What were they fighting about?"

"I couldn't hear. Our room's on the third floor."

The wolf scratched another note. "You share a room with…"

"Abby. Abigail Rose. The rabbit—she's the housemaid and she attends to Mrs St. Clair." There was nothing unusual about two female servants sharing a room, but Ellie felt compelled to add, "Flora, the other housemaid—she has the room adjoining ours."

For several seconds, while the wolf made notes, Ellie cursed herself. Why had she gone out of her way to point out where Flora lived? In all her police books, the criminals had tripped themselves up by talking too much. Not that she was a criminal or had anything—very much—to hide. But she resolved to give shorter answers. *Get a hold of yourself, El,* she said sternly in her mother's voice. *You're no good to Abby if you go to pieces.*

The wolf's ears flicked toward her again around his stiff blue hat. "Did the St. Clairs keep any valuables in the house?"

"Oh, well..." Ellie tried to think. "There's the good silver. We don't use that so often. Mrs St. Clair has some jewellery, of course. I don't know of anything else."

"Have there been break-ins before?"

"Oh, no. Not in the years I've been here."

The badger leaned forward. "Can you think of any reason someone might want to kill Mr Giles St. Clair?"

Ellie didn't want to mention his affair with Abby, or the business with Hope down in the village, so she said, "Well, sir, I don't know very much about his business, but I understand Mr Trevayn was here for a very important meeting. They were going to sell White Rose—that's the company he owns. It's an electronics firm. I suppose if someone wanted to stop that deal, they might have to kill him."

It was startling to her that she could say those words, "kill him," and not feel the weight of them. If she thought of herself as a character in one of the police books she'd read, it was easier to forget the intimate, intrusive smell of the blood, the languid spreading of it across the step, the look on Mr St. Clair's muzzle. She didn't have to wonder which of the people she'd spent the last four years with had pulled a gun and shot the master of the house.

Though of course, she hadn't spent four years with all of them. Flora had come on three years ago, and Abby had been hired when Rosalie, a pert young mouse, had unwisely let slip in front of Miss Kitt that she was bedding the master while the missus was in the town. Rosalie had often given little thought to what she was saying and couldn't read people the way Abby could.

Abby. Ellie wished she could see Abby, make sure the rabbit was doing all right. She was sensitive, and even if she hated Mr St. Clair...

Did she hate him enough to kill him?

The wolf was saying something, but Ellie didn't hear. She said, "Excuse me. Was it Mr St. Clair's gun that shot him?"

The wolf and badger both stared at her. "How do you know he had a gun?" the badger asked.

"We all knew." Ellie felt more comfortable here. "He went hunting sometimes, and had Donald fetch his guns. Donald told us he had a shotgun and a handgun. I don't know much other than that."

The wolf took over again. "Do you know why he kept a handgun?"

Ellie shook her head. "Perhaps he was worried about burglars."

"Perhaps." The badger drew out the word. "Perhaps. Currently we believe Mr St. Clair surprised a burglar, who shot him. But it is true that we have not been able to locate Mr St. Clair's gun yet."

The wolf scribbled something else on his pad. "Might've easily searched the deceased's room, found the gun, come out and shot him. Mr St. Clair was just coming back to his room when he was shot." He looked up. "Do you know why he was up so early?"

"I suppose he had a meeting," Ellie said. "But I don't know exactly. I was just preparing breakfast as I was supposed to."

"Right." The sergeant made one more note, then looked at the inspector. "Anything else, sir?"

The badger shook his head ponderously. "Please remain on the grounds until we have concluded our investigation, Miss Stone."

"Yessir," Ellie said.

•

It was lunchtime before Ellie got to see Abby. Flora had just taken the cucumber sandwiches and toast squares with paté out to the front of the house—the family did not want to eat inside even though the day was slightly overcast—when Abby came hurrying into the kitchen. Miss Turner spared one glance at the dishevelled, wide-eyed rabbit and said, "Oh, Flora's forgotten the honey. Miss Mary's sure to want it." She took a small jar of honey and walked out into the breezeway.

Abby threw her arms around Ellie, and the weasel hugged her back. "Oh, it's awful," Abby said. "Mrs Kate wouldn't stop crying, and it wasn't the carrying on, it was just the quiet kind where her fur got all wet. I tried to hold her, but I don't know if it did any good. And Master John and Miss Mary were there, but Master John just kept talking about how they were going to 'find the murderer,' and if you ask me, that just made it worse. And Miss Mary wasn't crying, but she didn't know what to say any more than I did. Oh, Ellie."

She lay her head on Ellie's shoulder, and the weasel stroked down the back of her head. "Shh," she said. "You did right by her. I'm sure your being there was a great comfort."

"Who could've done such a horrible thing?" Abby said. "Poor Mr Giles. I said all those terrible things about him yesterday. I wish I could take them back."

"He didn't hear you, I'm certain." Ellie kissed the base of Abby's ear.

"I heard them. And you heard them." Abby lifted her head, and her eyes were wide.

"What is it?"

"Oh." Abby's eyes slid away from Ellie's. "Do you think I should have told the police about…" Her voice lowered to a whisper. "About the times he…you know…"

"I suppose you ought," Ellie said, wrapping the rabbit in a hug. "But I don't know if I would have the strength to."

"After all," Abby went on, her voice cracking slightly, "then they might think it was Mrs Kate killed him, and I know it wasn't her."

Flora came into the kitchen just then, and though she wasn't humming a tune, she still bustled with energy. "Wasn't whom?"

Ellie and Abby broke apart, Abby dabbing at her eyes. "Mrs Kate," the rabbit said.

"Are we trying to solve the mystery, then?" Flora hurried over and lowered her voice to a whisper. "Ripping. I think it's got to be Trevayn. With Mr Giles dead, he takes over control of the company." She looked at Ellie. "You've read all those novels. What do you think?"

"The police say it was a burglar," Ellie said slowly.

"Oh, balderdash," Flora said. "It's never a burglar. Here, Ab, have my handkerchief."

The rabbit took the handkerchief and blew her nose. "I'm sorry," she said. "I'm just being silly."

"You haven't had a chance to cry properly," Ellie said. "Go on. I had a cry earlier. I'll miss him."

Abby leaned on the weasel and held the handkerchief up to her nose. "You always make me feel better. I know you'll take care of things."

"So, El." Flora's bright eyes caught hers. "What do you say? I bet you can solve the mystery before those police. That Inspector doesn't half look daft."

"I don't know." Ellie spoke slowly, turning it over in her head. "How do you know Trevayn takes over the company? Mr Giles—" Saying his name was hard. "His shares might go to Mrs Kate."

"Oooh." Flora brightened. "D'you reckon the sale is off? That'd clinch it for Trevayn."

"You'd know better than I. Where is he?"

"In the study. Nobody's gone out today. Respect for the deceased. But really, who else could it be but Trevayn or the missus?"

It seemed as though Mrs St. Clair would be the primary suspect. They'd argued, and Mr Giles was having at least two affairs. But Abby'd spent the morning with her, and the rabbit was still sobbing against Ellie, so Ellie put her sharp mind to work to change the subject. "Where was Miss Kitt in the morning?" she said, slowly.

"Old Stiff Upper Lip?" Flora clapped her paws together. "Don't know. She was there by the time I got downstairs, and was just going to call the police."

"But why on Earth would Miss Kitt…?" Abby rubbed at her eyes and took a breath, recovering, then offered the handkerchief back to Flora.

"Keep it," Flora said generously. "Anyway, he used to run around with her, a long while ago. Perhaps she found out about you like she did Roselie."

"She only had Roselie sacked," Ellie pointed out.

"Not to mention that Hope whatever-her-name-is in the village. Couldn't very well sack her, could she? Perhaps she got desperate."

"I still think that one's odd." Ellie rubbed her whiskers.

"Oh, I know." Flora turned as Miss Turner came back into the kitchen. "I mean, why take that chance when he was already getting…" She caught herself and reached out to Abby's shoulder. "Sorry, Ab."

"Speaking of," Miss Turner said, as though she'd been part of the conversation all along, "Master John's gone very cold to Mr Trevayn."

"Master John would be Mister St. Clair now, wouldn't he?" Abby said softly.

Silence reigned in the kitchen. "Yes," Miss Turner went on. "Well. Mr Trevayn wants to go ahead and have his business meeting today, and Master John—Mr St. Clair—said, 'I think you can wait one day out of respect for the dead,' and Mr Trevayn said as how the economic realities respected the living more than the dead, and Mrs Kate said she agreed with her son and Mr Trevayn made a comment about females and business sense and Mister John told him if he were going to be disrespectful, he could go have his luncheon elsewhere. That settled things down. Nothing like taking a fellow's food to put him in his place."

"What a horrid person," Abby said. "I'm not surprised he's not married yet."

"He has a lady friend," Flora put in. "He was talking all lovey to her on the phone."

"What sort of lady would allow him to touch her?"

Ellie remembered Trevayn's grip on her wrist, and changed the subject. "What did Miss Mary say?"

"Oh, she kept her eyes down. Poor girl."

"She and Master—Mister John were talking last night, after supper. Mister John was kicked out of college, Miss Mary said."

"I knew it," said Miss Turner. "What for?"

But Ellie hadn't heard, and so the three of them speculated, until Flora said, "What if it was for…something violent?"

"Our Master John?" Miss Turner waved a paw and left the group, pulling meat from the refrigerator and bringing it to the sideboard. "He wouldn't never."

"You're remembering little Master John the cub before he went off to school," Ellie said. "I only knew him a year before he went. He gashed that other fox's finger, remember? Mr St. Clair—Mister Giles—had to pay for the stitches."

"Ooh." Flora covered her mouth. "Is that why he was sent off to America?"

"No." Ellie looked at Miss Turner, who glanced back at her and then continued pounding the steaks flat with her iron mallet. "As I understand, he wanted to go. Mr Giles wanted him to go to Oxford, was it? But he didn't get in?"

"Didn't even apply," Miss Turner said. "He applied to this school in America and there was a frightful row about it. Mr Giles carried on about the quality of a good British education, and the schools they'd sent him to, and John said now he could make up his own mind, he was going to go somewhere he'd be happy. In the end they paid for him to go."

"You remember that very well," Flora said.

Miss Turner smiled, perking up her whiskers. "It was quite the loudest row they've had here. It went on for the better part of two weeks."

"And now he's had to come back."

"Poor Mister John." Abby sighed.

"Well, who do you think did it, Miss Turner?" Flora leaned back against the refrigerator.

"None of us in this kitchen, I suppose. There's no good us making up fanciful stories when we don't know anything." She attacked the next steak with fervour. "Haven't you got rooms to clean?"

"Police have sealed them up. Looking for evidence."

That gave Ellie an idea. "Miss Turner, do you need me for the next hour? I was thinking if Abby needs to stay with Mrs St. Clair, that maybe I could help Flora do the rooms. When the police are done, there won't be much time, and there's only her and Miss Kitt."

They all contemplated for a moment the likelihood of Miss Kitt stooping to do any actual work. When Miss Turner still hesitated, Flora said, "We could talk to the police about when the rooms are going to be done. They might tell us what they've been working on."

Though this was highly unlikely, it did the job. The plump weasel's ears perked up. "Well," she said thoughtfully. "Dinner's simple. I'll need you to do the potatoes, but no, go on."

Ellie, Flora, and Abby left via the back hallway. "Good thinking," Ellie whispered to Flora.

"Oh," the otter said, "she'd cook all the meals herself if someone brought her the news regularly. You should do it more often."

"I like cooking." Ellie squeezed Abby's paw. "You've been quiet."

"Have I? Oh, I'm sorry." Abby squeezed back, but distractedly.

As they passed the drawing-room, all three slowed automatically, but the room was silent. Flora and Abby, being the regular housemaids and not of the species of any of the guests, went through the drawing-room to find the police while Ellie waited, thinking, mostly about Abby.

The rabbit was sweet, and Ellie worried that murder would take a toll on that. She thought about how Abby had objected to Mr St. Clair taking his time with her while his wife was at the house (and that was odd, Ellie had to admit, but then, Mrs St. Clair had actually missed the Orphans Aid Society meeting and the Ladies' Works meeting at the church this past week, so she'd not been out of the house, and maybe Mr St. Clair, like so many males of any species, just couldn't wait). Abby didn't particularly enjoy his attentions, true, but she'd spared time to worry about the feelings of the missus, and that was one of the things Ellie loved about her. How would that spirit survive in a house where something as callous and brutal as a murder had taken place?

•

"Abby's gone for a lie down," Flora said. "She told me to tell you not to worry about her. The police said they're done with the west wing, so we can go through and clean. Let's start with Mr Trevayn's room."

The stoat was occupying the primary guest room, a spacious suite looking out over the front of the house rather than the gardens that included a study as well as a bedroom. He had only been staying there two days, but already his scent permeated the study when Ellie and Flora walked in.

"Well, we'll have to get the lavender in here when he goes." Flora waved a paw in front of her nose. "Goodness. Weasels, I swear. Oh, I'm sorry, El. It's not *all* weasels. Your bedroom doesn't smell this strong. It's the male scent, isn't it? Oh, he's made a proper mess of the coverings on the divan."

She hurried to the couch, but Ellie stopped her, closing the door to the suite. "Wait! We must look around and see exactly how things look."

Flora stopped with one paw stretched out toward a lace cover that had fallen from the armrest. "What, you want to investigate?" Her expression went from startled to conspiratorial in no time flat. "You think the position of this cover might be significant?"

"It might." Ellie walked over to the desk, which was catching the afternoon sun. "But here's where the business papers are."

"We're not to touch business papers," Flora said. "Mr St. Clair is always quite clear on that."

"We won't touch them, then. But look." Ellie went over to the desk. "There's one article out of the stack here."

On the desk, two envelopes on official-looking stationery lay opened, but with the folded letters still inside them. Ellie thought about pulling the letters out, but that would likely be noticeable when Mr Trevayn came back. She did note the return address: both were from BOAC. BOAC, she thought. Airplanes, perhaps? To the right side of the desk was a series of reprints, articles torn out of magazines or official reprints with the header "NOT FOR SALE" on them. Flora and Ellie bent over the one that lay askew on the desk.

"'Predicted Fluctuation In Transistor Markets'? I don't understand what this means at all. Is there a market like Enfield's where they sell transistors?"

Ellie studied the words. "I believe it just means people buying and selling transistors, and I suppose the prices fluctuate—"

"But what might this have to do with the murder?" The otter hissed the words.

"Maybe nothing. Maybe."

Flora frowned and then bent down to the paper. "It smells like…" She looked up. "Fox."

Ellie bent down as well. The trace was faint, but she caught the musky scent. "Can you tell which one?"

"Mmm. No." Flora sniffed again and shook her head.

They straightened and looked at each other. "Whoever it was could've been in here at any time, though."

"Not since the police closed it up."

"It would make sense that he might want to show Mr St. Clair the article, I suppose." Ellie rubbed her whiskers.

"Maybe there's a fresher scent somewhere else."

But though they sniffed carefully around the room, they found nothing but the strong smell of stoat. "He's a careless one," Flora said as Ellie straightened the covers on the divan and began sweeping the carpet. "Oh! Shouldn't we be looking for a gun?"

"Oh." Ellie had put the gun out of her mind, feeling sure that that was what had splashed into the garden pond. "Yes, although I'm sure the police have looked. They wouldn't miss a gun."

"Don't know." Flora sniffed. "That inspector looked rather dim. The young wolf looked clever, though. Cooke, his name was, wasn't it? You think he's married?"

"You could ask him."

"Handsome, police, probably draws a nice salary." Flora bustled into the bedroom. "What do you think police make these days?"

Ellie hurried after her. "Don't touch anything!"

"Oh, there's nothing in here but bedclothes and a wardrobe."

"There's his suitcase," Ellie pointed out.

"It's closed."

The weasel shot a look at the otter, who was wringing her small paws. "But not locked," Ellie said, working a claw under the lid.

But sadly, the suitcase held only a business suit, underclothes, and a novel by Norman Mailer. Beneath the novel there was an envelope from what looked like a law firm, but it was sealed. "He'll smell you in there," Flora said.

"I'm barely touching the clothes and I smell like him anyway." There was no false bottom in the suitcase, nor secret compartment where compromising letters might be hidden. Ellie sighed and closed the suitcase. "Anything in the wardrobe?"

"No, nor on it neither." Flora stood on tiptoe and dusted along the top of the large antique furnishing. "Just his suit."

There was no more scent of fox in the bedroom as far as they could tell. Ellie made the bed and while Flora continued dusting the telephone on the night table, took the flowers out of the vase behind it, and cleaned out the bathroom. "We'll replace the flowers later," Flora said. "Now for suspect number two."

As they crossed the hall, Ellie made an effort not to look down it to the landing where Giles St. Clair had lain sprawled that morning. Out of the corner of her eye, she saw the white cloth there, and had the impression that the body was gone, but she kept her head forward and stepped quickly after Flora's thick tail.

Unlike Mr Trevayn, John occupied a single room, albeit a large one, with the bed below one window and the writing desk below the other. They went to the writing desk first, which, like Mr Trevayn's, was piled with papers. But these were not magazine articles or reprints; these were international newspapers, and they were not strewn about the desk; they were stacked neatly.

"I had no idea Eldridge's stocked the International Herald Tribune," Ellie murmured.

Flora picked up a New York Times. "They still come over on the boat, I see. This one is a month old." She perused the front page. "Good heavens, they are very blunt over there."

The room smelled strongly of fox, but Ellie could not tell whether it was the same scent that had lingered faintly around Mr Trevayn's desk. She wanted to keep investigating like a detective, but she had no idea what she was looking for. Something people were hiding, yes, but where? John, unlike Mr Trevayn, knew the house well, so perhaps at the back of the closet?

Flora continued to read, while Ellie straightened up the rest of the room, with a sharp eye out for potential hiding places. In making the bed, she leaned down to look beneath it, as she had done in Mr Trevayn's room, and just as in the other room, there was nothing there. But in getting up, she stepped on a floorboard that shifted under her weight.

"Flora," Ellie hissed. "Come here!"

She dug her claws under the edge of the boards while the otter came over. "Oh," Flora said. "Loose floorboards?"

Ellie pried up the first board easily, and then another. In the space below them was a glossy wooden case the size of a breadbox. The weasel pulled it up into the light, and she and Flora stared.

"Open it," Flora whispered.

"It's locked." Ellie looked up at the otter. "This is what I think it is, though, isn't it?"

Flora nodded. "Mr St. Clair has one just like it. It's a case for a gun."

•

While they were finishing Mary's room, Miss Kitt found them. "Elsinore," she said. "Miss Turner requires your help in the kitchen."

"Yes'm," Ellie said. She exchanged a "we shall talk later" look with Flora. They had replaced the locked gun case below John's floorboard, but had not discussed whether to go to the police with the evidence.

As they left the room, Miss Kitt turned right and made her way down the hallway toward the grand stair. Ellie hesitated, but the roe deer waved her imperiously forward. "Mr Trevayn has gone out. You may come down this way."

Ellie hesitated, and then walked forward. Just before the stairs, she glanced to her right, out to the terrace. Impossibly, it had been less than twelve hours since she'd stood there watching the sun rise, and then had heard the shattering explosion. Mr St. Clair would have been standing just a few feet in front of her, facing the east wing just as she was doing now. And someone had been standing in front of him, someone he knew, someone he had never expected to produce a revolver and fire it…

"Come on, girl," Miss Kitt snapped from halfway down the stair.

Ellie blinked and hurried down, keeping to the edge of the white sheet laid over the landing to make sure she didn't tread on anywhere poor Mr St. Clair's blood had been. As she reached the bottom, Sergeant Cooke opened the study door and came out. "Ah, Miss Stone," the wolf said, and when Miss Kitt turned sharply, he held up a paw and smiled. "Sorry to deprive you of your assistant cook, Miss Kitt, but we had one or two more questions for her, if you don't mind."

Miss Kitt stared at him. Ellie heard from inside the study the voice of Mrs St. Clair: "…has gone out. I assure you I may answer any questions regarding the disposition of White Rose."

She sounded weary, and Ellie wished she could go in and take her mistress's paw, just to give her comfort for a moment. Of course, Ellie was terrible at that sort of thing. Abby was much better at it.

"I suppose," Miss Kitt said finally, "she can be spared for a short time." She emphasised the last two words. "I will inform Miss Turner that her help will be delayed. One hopes that supper will not also be."

Abby—Ellie hoped she was having a nice rest upstairs. She followed the young wolf to the drawing-room. Behind her, she heard Mrs St. Clair say, in a very different voice, a colder one, "Oh, is that so? No, I was not aware—"

And then she was in the drawing-room, the door closed carefully behind her. "I don't think Miss Kitt likes us much," the wolf observed.

"There's been so much disruption. First Master John coming home, then Mr Trevayn, and then..." Ellie cast her eyes around the empty room. "Where's the Inspector?"

"He's searching the gardens." The wolf smiled. "Please have a seat."

She sat in one of the Louis XIV chairs, unable to match his smile. "Am I in trouble?"

The officer took a chair next to hers and produced his pad and paper again. "Is there something you should be in trouble for?"

Ellie had read in her police novels that the best lies were short and simple, and she put this into practice. "No."

"Then you're not." The wolf took a pencil from his pocket. "But you were awake before the rest of the household, is that right?"

"Yes." She didn't venture any more than that.

"What time?"

"Well, it was before sunrise. I suppose it must have been about half past four. I set the fires on the first floor, and then—and then went to the kitchen to prepare breakfast."

"There are no second-floor rooms that require fires?"

Ellie flattened her ears. "I was going to do them after the breakfast. I don't normally set fires and it took me longer than I'd thought."

"Mm." The wolf made a note. "The kitchen is just off the servants' entrance on that side of the house, is that right?" She nodded. "Did you see anyone come in or leave by that door?"

"No." It was rather truthful; she hadn't seen herself come in or leave. She doubted the distinction would hold up before a jury, especially as she'd already lied about where she'd been. "Do you think—was there someone else in the house?"

"The Inspector thinks it might have been a burglar. But we haven't found any forced windows or doors. So it's possible it was someone who was granted access to the house. You didn't let someone else in, did you?"

His tone was conversational but the question was sharp. "No, sir," Ellie replied emphatically.

"Do you know anyone else who might have access to the house? Tradesfolk, anyone?"

"The squirrels from the dairy come up, but they hadn't come yet that day." She focused her mind on recalling the details of the house's interaction with the village. "And Mr Trumbull the baker, he sometimes comes up early."

"But he hadn't come up either."

"No, sir."

"Right. Do you know anyone in the village who might have any reason to come up to the house in the early hours?"

Ellie shook her head. "You mean, to kill Mr St. Clair?" She was proud of the way her voice remained steady.

"Well, possibly." The wolf put his pencil away. "But the Inspector rather thinks it was someone come up to steal something. Didn't expect Mr St. Clair to be walking around, was startled, and..."

The drawing-room door swung open. Kate St. Clair stood there, and as Ellie looked up, she thought that this was a very different Mrs Kate from the one she'd seen this morning, weeping. This was—she thought of a time last year when there'd been a fellow from the village who'd been a trifle too insistent on visiting Miss Mary, and when Mrs St. Clair had told him in no uncertain terms to leave her daughter in peace, she had worn an expression very like this one. Her ears were straight up and her nose lifted; she stood ramrod-straight and her tail curled very properly behind her, as still as the rest of her. Her tone, though, was not passionate, but very calm and restrained. "Sergeant," she said. "I wonder if I might trouble you for a moment."

The wolf rose to his feet, and Ellie followed suit. "I wonder," Mrs St. Clair continued, "if you remember at what time this morning you were summoned to Tremontaine."

"Ma'am, it was..." The wolf checked his pad. "We arrived here at six forty-five, and it is about fifteen minutes to get up here from the village. I haven't noted the time of the phone call here—we have it back at the station—but I do remember noting it wasn't quite six-thirty when we left. Six-twenty at the earliest, I would say."

"Thank you," she said. She turned to leave, and then paused with one paw on the door. "How is your investigation proceeding?"

Her eyes travelled to Ellie, so that the weasel ducked away from the gaze. The wolf did not notice, but looked at his pad. "We are looking into the possibility of a burglar from the village. Constable Wood is making inquiries as to whether anyone was seen on the road from Tremontaine to the village between the hours of five and seven this morning."

"I see." Mrs St. Clair's eyes looked distant for a moment.

The wolf coughed, his own tail curling to a more proper angle. "Would it be possible to assemble the staff and ask them?"

For a moment, the vixen appeared not to have heard the question. Then her ears flicked and she turned her head. "Miss Kitt should be able to do that for you."

"Yes. Ah. Miss Kitt has said that the running of the household must proceed and that she cannot countenance a disruption..."

"What nonsense." Mrs St. Clair raised a paw. "Certainly we wish to cooperate in whatever manner possible with the police. If any of the servants knows anything that might help..."

"The Inspector and I would be most obliged," Cooke said. "It's only that interviewing them one at a time takes so long. And it's only for one question."

Ellie swallowed and felt twin blushes of shame and relief. Yes, she was hiding something, but they hadn't singled her out—they were interrogating everyone on staff. But surely it was rather unusual to ask a question of everyone in a room together. She had not heard of police doing that before. Was it really to save time? Or was it, perhaps, so that they could see if someone flicked an ear toward someone else—if someone revealed that they knew more than they were telling?

•

The Inspector strode with the same ponderousness of his speech. His steps thudded along the main hallway floor as he walked up in front of the assembled staff. The family, too, had assembled, though the younger foxes sat together on the chaise longue with their tails curled beside them on the cushions, John still looking like a shocked son and not very much like the new head of the household. Their mother, cool and collected, stood next to them. Mr Trevayn, who had returned from his errand, leaned against the wall apart from the family.

Ellie had protested that she'd already answered the questions, but the wolf had said apologetically that the Inspector would like to ask her, so she stood stiffly next to Miss Turner, with Flora on her next side and Abby beyond her, rubbing her eyes. Donald stood beside Abby, uncomfortably, looking down at the floor. To Miss Turner's right stood Miss Kitt, and Mr Pearson the elegant brown rat held down the end of the line.

"I will keep this brief," the badger said, stopping to look at the row of staff. "We have reason to believe that the person who shot Mr St. Clair came from outside the house sometime between five and five-thirty in the morning. Mr St. Clair surprised them and they subsequently shot him once. We have recovered Mr St. Clair's gun from the pond in the garden."

Ellie remembered the thing that had flown past her, the splash, her squeak.

"We believe the murderer fled down the terrace stairs, threw the gun into the pond, and then returned to the village. Now, I require a small piece of information to assist my deductive method. Does any of you know any person who might have visited the house between five and six this morning?"

A small gasp came from Ellie's left. She didn't think it was Flora, but had it been Abby or Donald? The Inspector, watching them, would know, but Ellie couldn't tell.

"Flora," Miss Kitt said, "you were laying the fires. Did you hear anyone?"

The otter turned and met Ellie's eyes. Ellie spoke up. "Beg your pardon, Miss Kitt, but I laid the fires because Flora'd done the washing-up for me the night before."

The roe deer glared down over Miss Turner's head, past Ellie, to Flora. "Why was I not informed of this?"

"Sorry, ma'am," Flora said. "Ellie's done the fires before and I knew she'd do a good job of it."

"And how did you spend your morning?" Inspector Bennett asked.

"Sleeping, sir." Flora faced him. "Until I was woken up by that explosion."

Before Ellie turned back to the Inspector as well, she glanced past the line of staff to the family. Mrs St. Clair was staring fixedly at nothing, it seemed. Miss Mary had her paws in her lap and was keeping her ears down. Mister John—it was still hard not to think of him as "Master John"—and Mr Trevayn were both staring right at Ellie. Or perhaps Flora? Ellie straightened, looking forward, and with a shock noticed Sergeant Cooke's eyes fixed on her.

"You didn't meet someone from the village?" the Inspector continued to Flora.

"No, sir."

The badger's gaze swept the rest of them. "None of the rest of you saw anyone in the house who is not in this room right now?"

"No, sir," they chorused.

"Very well." He looked up and down the line and tapped his head just below the ear. "Thank you. I think I have discovered what I need to know."

A knock came at the door. The young wolf opened it to admit a police constable, a goat. "Beggin' your pardon, sir, but I found something."

"Oh?" The inspector turned and made his way toward the door.

Before he got there, the goat held up a piece of paper. "Yes, sir. It was that wolf, Hope."

•

The Inspector had silenced the constable, but not before the room was set to murmuring, shocked looks on everyone's muzzle. Ellie looked swiftly around the room to see people's reactions, and came around to Abby staring at her, her ears down. The line of staff had broken down even though they'd not been officially dismissed, so Ellie hurried to Abby's side and took her paw.

"I'm so ashamed," Abby said, but when Ellie asked her why, she wouldn't say more.

Miss Kitt's imperious voice cut through the commotion. "Flora, Donald, I believe the dining room must be prepared. Marjorie, Ellie, supper must be ready in one hour. Abby, the upstairs rooms need turning down."

Ellie squeezed Abby's paw and patted it. "Never mind, old soul," she said, and Abby's eyes lit gratefully. "Go on. I'll just be down here and we'll catch up tonight."

"Thanks," Abby said, and she turned for the large foyer and the grand staircase.

Miss Turner had already made her way to the kitchen with a gesture to Ellie to follow. Flora exchanged a wink with Ellie as she hurried off behind Donald, the dhole's tail curled even further than usual under his legs. Ellie walked slowly toward the kitchen, listening as Mrs St. Clair made her way over to the police.

"What is to be done with this 'Hope' person?" she asked.

There was a pause, and then the badger replied. "We have only one account, from…"

The sheep said, "Devin Wright, baker. He's a fox. Excellent night vision."

"I know Mister Wright well." The vixen's voice could have chilled ice. "Have you any motive for Hope to be at the house?"

A longer pause. "Not yet, ma'am."

"I would feel much safer were she in custody tonight," Mrs St. Clair said.

"But—"

The young wolf's protest lasted only one word. The badger interrupted. "Of course, ma'am, we can bring her in for questioning. Sergeant, see to it."

"Yes, sir." The wolf responded crisply, and Ellie, glimpsing Miss Kitt's foreboding eye turned in her direction, hurried to the kitchen.

"Well?" Miss Turner greeted her with a question and a tray of sweetbreads. "What of this Hope? It's his mistress, isn't it? Think she came here for revenge?"

"Revenge?" Ellie took the tray and set it down, going to the pantry for flour. "For what? If he was…carrying on with her—"

"Please!" The portly weasel fluttered a paw. "If poor Mr Giles was seen in the company of someone young and female, well then, he was certainly enjoying that company." She applied herself to the sauce bubbling on the stove. "And you knew Hope a little, didn't you?"

"Talked to her once or twice." Ellie carried the flour over to the sweetbreads and set out a dish. "But she just didn't seem like the type to take on with—with Mr St. Clair."

"Then what was she doing coming up here middle of the night?" Miss Turner removed the wooden spoon and gestured with it. "You mark my words, he told her it was over and she shot him."

"Oh, Miss Turner."

"You have seen the way Miss Kitt looks at him? Still, after all these years?"

Ellie coated the sweetbreads in flour and sighed. "Miss Kitt never shot him."

"She finds excuses to send away any girl in this household he takes up with." Miss Turner resumed her stirring. "And she's not a wolf. Different temperament, those wolves. Get me the rosemary, would you? Oh, Flora, are they wanting the cucumber salad already?"

But it was not the small otter who had come through the breezeway from the dining room, though Ellie had at first made the same mistake. "I'm sorry to disturb you," Mr Trevayn said, and both Ellie and Miss Turner froze.

Miss Turner recovered first. "You ought not to be here, sir," she said.

"Oh, custom be damned," the stoat said. "It causes me no offence to see my fellow weasels in the service of another, any more than it would trouble…" A shadow flickered over his muzzle, and he crossed the kitchen to Ellie. "In fact, the custom has deprived me of the opportunity to make the acquaintance of this lovely young thing. Your name is Stone, I believe?"

"Elsinore Stone, yes sir." Ellie's throat felt dry. Her paws were white with flour and sticky with sweetbreads, and she gave a brief thanks that the smell of the viands was so strong. All she could imagine was that Mr Trevayn had caught her scent in his room, and she hoped he would not be able to place it well in the confusion of other scents.

"They call you Ellie, is that right?"

"Yes, sir."

"Miss Turner." He addressed the cook, who had taken out some cucumbers to chop and appeared to be trying to drown out his presence with sharp strikes of the knife blade. "Might I steal Ellie for a short conversation?"

The chopping paused. "Of course, sir. You're a guest in the house and if Mrs Kate said it was all right, well, it's not my place to say no."

Mr Trevayn's polite smile was fixed on his face, his whiskers pert and upright, and his dark eyes reflected the flickers of light from the stove. Ellie felt sure he had not asked Mrs St. Clair's permission. "It won't be long, I promise. If the miss does not object?" He extended a paw.

She didn't want to be alone with him, but the curiosity about what he wanted to talk about burned her as strongly as she could see it did Miss Turner, whose short tail twitched from side to side. So Ellie held up her floury fingers. "Let me wash," she said.

"Of course." He pointed to the door that led to the hall and the servants' entrance. "I'll meet you just outside, shall I?"

When he'd gone, there followed a hastily whispered conversation between Miss Turner and Ellie, in which Miss Turner asked Ellie to tell her anything suspicious she'd seen in the room when she cleaned it, in case, she said darkly, "you don't come back."

Ellie did not quite believe Mr Trevayn was artless enough to ask her out in front of a witness and then murder her, but she did wonder if he might not be planning to threaten her, and she did not know how she would react in that case. What if he knew she'd gone through his suitcase?

"I'll meet you just outside, shall I?"

Or had smelled her at his desk? She hadn't looked at any of the letters, but now she wished she had.

But she told Miss Turner about the smell of fox on the magazine article, about the letters from BOAC, and about the letter from the law firm. "Transistors," Miss Turner said, her muzzle wrinkling. "That's what White Rose makes, isn't it?"

"It's related to what they make." Ellie dried her paws and gestured to the refrigerator in the kitchen. "All these things have transistors in them."

"Well, go and find out what you can from him. Don't let him ask all the questions. And don't turn your back on him, mind."

With that instruction in her ears, Ellie hurried out the servants' entrance and found the stoat waiting for her on the white gravel path. The crunch of it under her feet reminded her of that morning, but she steeled herself against the feeling of panic, reminding herself that she was being a detective, and walked quickly over to him.

He wore the same shirt and tie he'd been wearing that morning, though somewhat more rumpled. The cuffs of the shirt had been turned up his wrists and small patches of sweat stained the shirt. He did not offer her his arm again, but began walking along the path, past the hawthorn hedges on the left and the peonies planted against the house to the right. "Such a lovely garden," he murmured.

"Yes, sir," Ellie said, and then screwed up her courage. "Did your errand today meet with success?"

He turned and measured her with his gaze. "Yes. Yes, I fancy you could say that."

"I don't mean to pry," she said. "I was just making conversation."

"Yes. Well, it will depend on a telephone call tomorrow, but I anticipate everything going my way." She heard the word "finally" at the end of the sentence even though he did not say it.

"I'm glad to hear it, sir."

"Thank you, Ellie. As it happens, if everything does go my way, I will come into a considerable fortune, and that is partly what I wanted to talk to you about."

"You inherited Mr St. Clair's shares, sir?" The words burst out before she could stop them.

"Good heavens, no. I mean, unless he made provisions in a will he did not tell me about. No, his wife inherits his shares, but I believe this tragedy needn't prevent all of us from making a good deal of money."

"That's good to hear, sir."

"You would think so, would you not? Ellie, if I told you I had spent the better part of today ensuring that you would live out the rest of your days without worrying about money, you'd thank me, would you not?"

She thought the question rhetorical, but he did not go on, so after a moment, she said, "Yes, sir, I would."

"Yes." He kicked at a small dark stone, sending it skittering away from the white. His toes flexed as he set his foot down again. "It's all worth it, I suppose."

They rounded the corner of the house. The lily pond and larger flower garden came into view, dark under the towering shadow of Tremontaine's gables. Ellie's steps faltered at the sight of the pond, and then she looked to her right at the grassy verge. She couldn't make out any footprints there, although she was certain the gardener had not come today. So perhaps nobody would have been able to tell she had been there this morning.

"Was that what you wanted to ask me, sir?"

"Hm? Oh, no." The stoat stopped just short of the lily pond, looking ahead to where the large terrace rose ahead of them. He turned to Ellie, his voice pleasant, his smile fixed. "I wanted to ask you why you lied to the police."

For a moment, the bright sky overhead and the raucous colours of the flower garden convinced Ellie that she must have misheard. The day was too ordinary, too real for a question like that. Then the words sunk in and she drew in a gasp before reminding herself that she was a detective. "What makes you think I lied?" she asked. "Sir."

Mr Trevayn's voice lost none of its pleasantness. His dark eyes remained impenetrable. "Well, you said you never came up to the second floor. I overheard them talking about that. But I was coming out of my room, getting ready for our breakfast meeting, and I saw you there."

He'd seen her. She had looked to either side when she'd come up the stairs, but it was just possible that he had been looking out of his room, down the dark hallway, and he'd seen her. "Sir," she said, and then stopped, at a loss. He could easily be lying, trying to trap her.

"You must have come down through here," he said. "Down the terrace steps, around the side of the building. Just the path they say the murderer took."

"I didn't shoot Mr Giles." She kept her voice steady, angry.

"You must see it looks very bad for you." He kept that bland smile.

"But if you didn't, then why would you lie?" She didn't answer. "Could you be protecting someone? I believe you know that Hope person the police are after."

"I didn't see anything," she insisted. "What about you, sir? You were up as well. Did you not see the murderer?"

"Regrettably, no. I had just shown poor Giles a magazine article and was fetching my suit jacket when he left to see if Donald had brought the car around. I heard him greet someone, and then the shot, but by the time I came out from my bedroom into the hallway, whoever had shot him had left." He looked up at the terrace. "If only I'd thought to run out onto the terrace, but my first thought was for Giles. Alas, he was beyond my help."

Ellie didn't want to think of the morning again, now that the shot was associated in her mind with the horrible bloody body of Mr St. Clair. But something the stoat had said nagged at her, very slightly. Something that she'd forgotten, or not paid close enough attention to…no, it was gone now.

"It was a horrible thing," she said quietly. She wanted more than anything now to hurry back to the kitchen, to leave Mr Trevayn with his placid, unemotional expression and his dark eyes.

"Yes, horrible," he echoed. "Ellie, I didn't ask you out here to call you a liar. I am aware that there are often reasons one may not be completely frank with the police. In fact, I admire someone who can on occasion rely on her own judgment above custom. Such people are rare. In addition, I have been quite pleased with the quality of meals here, and once this deal is finalised, I will be looking to retain the services of a cook. I wonder if you might keep me in mind as a possible employer."

Again, the stark reality of the day overwhelmed the unreality of the words. Her mind reeled. To leave Tremontaine? "To be a head cook, sir?"

"Of course. At first I will only require one, but if, as I suspect, my new fortune brings me the prospect of a family, I am sure I will be able to hire you an assistant."

Though Ellie did not look up at the third floor, she felt Abby's presence there. "It is a generous offer, sir, but…I am quite content with my position at Tremontaine."

"Oh, come," he said. "I've yet to meet a junior person in any position who didn't want to rule the roost one day. I can assure you that if it is a modern kitchen you desire, I will be able to afford the same refrigerator old Giles—well, that they have here. Perhaps even two."

"Thank you, sir, but I cannot consider it now. One day in the future…" One day when Abby could come with her. And what could one possibly keep in two refrigerators, especially in a bachelor household?

Now, only now, he scowled. "I won't offer again," he said.

"Thank you, sir," Ellie repeated. "I very much appreciate the offer. I hope you won't take offence."

"Of course not." But his words were clipped and short and he turned on his heel and stalked away from her, up the terrace steps.

Ellie watched him enter the house. She was reminded of watching Mr and Mrs St. Clair have an argument in nearly this very spot, and she turned and hurried back to the house, eyes moist, before she could dwell on it.

●

"Offered you a position?" Miss Turner stared at her. "Well, how did he know what you'd cooked?"

That was a point Ellie hadn't thought of. "I don't know," she said. "I turned him down."

"Oh, not that you couldn't handle meals for a bachelor," Miss Turner said. "It's just not done, you know. Properly he should talk to Mrs St. Clair and Miss Kitt, get your references, and so on."

"Maybe he wanted to see if I would be interested. Though he did offer the position outright." Ellie had come back to find the sweetbreads nearly done, and was helping shell the peas now. "And anyway, he isn't supposed to see me at all anyway, so he can't be too beholden to custom."

"There is that." Miss Turner shelled peas with the same ruthless efficiency she brought to everything, her paws a blur. She slit the pea pod lengthwise with a claw, pulled the peas out with the same claw, and dropped the shell into the rubbish bin, all in about three seconds. "Why did you turn him down? It would be quite a step, at your age."

"I don't trust him," Ellie said in a low voice. "And besides, there's Abby."

"You won't always be able to work in the same house," Miss Turner said. "Best to save the staff romances for a senior position. Although with poor Mr Giles gone, I suppose Abby may stay longer than the previous housemaids. I could swear Mrs Kate hired them especially for Mr Giles's pleasure."

"Don't," Ellie said, feeling warmth in her ears. It was the first time Miss Turner had used the word "romance" to describe her relationship to

Abby, and hearing it without judgment felt good and strange all at the same time. And then, on the heels of it, being reminded that Mr St. Clair had used Abby at his leisure—well, it was not a pleasant association; that was all. Though it did soften her grief at his demise, and perhaps that was what Miss Turner had intended to do. She looked at the older weasel. "What about you and Mr Pearson?"

"We're senior, my dear, and anyway, it's not a romance. It's more like a marriage."

Her wry tone and words made Ellie laugh, and that, too, felt strange, but also good.

•

Flora had plenty to tell them as they washed up from dinner, leaning against the pantry while Ellie scrubbed the pots and Miss Turner did the plates and silver, and Abby dried them and put them on the rack on the sideboard. "If the conversation had been any colder, I shouldn't have needed to bring out ice," she chirped. "First it was Mrs Kate talking business with Mr Trevayn, and him not saying much back to her, but then she said 'I can call them just as well as you can, and they'll talk to me,' and so he told her he had met with the Bowack people..."

"BOAC," Ellie said. "That's who wrote the letters in his desk."

"Anyway, he seemed to think they would go ahead with the deal without Mr St. Clair, and Mrs St. Clair said he didn't have the shares to go ahead with it, and he said something about..." Flora screwed up her otter's muzzle and stuck her tongue out, concentrating, "the board would be on his side and her shares were un-voting? Something like that."

Nobody could shed any light on what this meant. After a moment, Flora went on. "I think," she said, "it was something to do with Mrs St. Clair being a lady, you know, and Mr Trevayn didn't quite say it, but it seemed he thought he would have the board's confidence more."

"Mr St. Clair certainly had a head for business," Miss Turner said.

Ellie felt that this was something of a betrayal of her gender. "I've known ladies had just as good heads on their shoulders."

"Oh, bless you, dear, of course. Mrs Kate just never showed much of an interest in business."

"She had newspapers in her room," Abby put in.

Flora clearly felt she was losing the spotlight. "That's what Mister John jumped in and said. He said his mother was very bright and kept up on current events better than Mr Trevayn did, he would wager, and Mr

Trevayn called him a brat, and Miss Mary came in and said, 'don't,' but real quiet, and that calmed things down a little."

"Was it business the whole night?" Miss Turner asked. Abby and Ellie kept quiet, though Ellie was relieved to see that Abby seemed more relaxed around her. When she gave a pot to Abby to dry, the rabbit's paw lingered on her wet, soapy one, and that was nice.

"They talked about arrangements for poor Mr St. Clair's funeral."

This cast a pall on the kitchen. Flora struggled gamely forward. "Mr Trevayn said he would bear the expense, and Mrs St. Clair snapped that he didn't need to. And then they talked about that poor Hope, and Mr Trevayn asked if Mrs St. Clair knew about her and Mr St. Clair until Mister John told him to be quiet. And Mrs St. Clair didn't say anything, but Miss Mary said she thought Hope was a nice girl and she couldn't believe she would do such a thing. Then Mister John said that people you thought were nice could be capable of just about anything and there were news stories all over about nice people doing terrible things, and that's just the way the world is."

"In America, maybe," Miss Turner sniffed.

"Oh, you didn't read about that poisoning case last year?"

"That's different, dear. She wasn't a nice person. Speaking of," Miss Turner turned with a wicked gleam in her eye, "how did Mister Trevayn like his potatoes? Did he think they were 'safe'?"

"Oh," Flora said, "he didn't say nothing about 'em. Ate them all, but I did see him dab at his eyes with a napkin."

"Maybe he'll learn before he makes more comments about my food." Miss Turner turned to Ellie. "Chilli sauce. You remember that when someone says you need to cook something 'exotic' or 'different.' One taste of that and they'll be quite content with a good English pudding. It's the little tricks that make one a successful head cook."

This brought a round of questions, interested from Flora and alarmed from Abby, about Ellie's head cook prospects, which both weasels put to rest quickly. Ellie recounted her interview with Mr Trevayn.

"I still don't know if he deserved the chilli sauce." Abby eyed the bright red bottle.

"It's a matter of cook's pride, dear. Speaking of—"

"You can put that in our meals anytime," Flora said. "Me and Donald, it makes us feel quite at home. My mum went through a bottle of that a month, just about."

"Is Mrs St. Clair all right?" Abby asked. "You said she was quiet."

"She ate well enough," Flora said. "She's asked me to sit up with her tonight. Says she don't feel safe in the house. I reckon she's covering up that she's lonely. She's proud, is Mrs Kate."

"Poor thing," Miss Turner said. "I know when my father passed, my mum just pined away for him. Only lasted two more months herself."

"Mrs St. Clair won't be passing on!" Abby sounded alarmed.

Ellie reached out a damp paw to squeeze the rabbit's wrist. "No, no. She just needs company for a little while."

"I would've sat up with her," Abby said.

"You were up with her all day today." Flora smiled. "I don't mind. I'll have a quick kip before bed so I can stay up."

"I'll make you a pot of coffee if you like," Abby offered.

"Tea's splendid." The otter jumped down and was at the pantry before Miss Turner could say anything. "I like Darjeeling. Have we got any?"

"No, and stay out of there." The portly weasel hurried over and closed the pantry, glaring at Flora. "It'll take me forever to get everything back where it belongs. Mrs Kate always takes tea before bed, so I'll just send up enough for two."

"Belongs." Flora rolled her eyes where only Ellie and Abby could see. "You can see and smell where everything is anyway."

In the ensuing silence, raised voices could be heard faintly from the direction of the hallway. "Ooh," Flora whispered. "Come on."

She hurried out into the servants' passage, and after a moment, Miss Turner followed. Alone in the kitchen, Ellie took a moment to kiss Abby, and then said, "Come on, I want to hear what's going on."

They joined Flora and Miss Turner in the passage, safely out of view of the drawing-room door. The conversation came easily to them in the still air of the hall over the faint strains of classical music. "What alternative is there?" John St. Clair was saying. "That someone in Tremontaine did it? Does the Inspector think that?"

The young police officer, Sergeant Cooke, answered. "Sir, the Inspector is of the opinion that Miss Cooper is the primary suspect. We understand it may be hard to believe, but we have a definite identification—"

"Oh, definite!" This was Mary's voice. "He saw someone wearing her clothing for five seconds along the road. It could have been almost anyone. It could have been you, Sergeant."

"I suppose so, ma'am; however, I was home at the time."

"Have *you* an alibi?" Mary asked. "And when is he supposed to have seen her on the road?"

"Early in the morning hours, well before sunrise. He wakes at four to begin baking, and he is sure it was not too long after that."

Abby elbowed Ellie, who spread her paws to indicate she hadn't seen anything to do with Hope.

"And when did he see her come back?"

"Oh, Mary, I'm sure the police have established all the particulars. Except for someone who actually witnessed the crime."

"Well, who was setting the fires that morning? Wouldn't Flora have been awake then?"

"I believe it was Miss Stone, and she has testified that she was on the first floor when she heard the shot." The wolf's voice was patient.

"Very convenient," Mary said.

"Mary, you're not honestly suggesting—"

"No, no. But my point is, it could have been anyone. Why should this Hope creature come all the way up here in the wee hours just to shoot Father?"

The servants' eyes gleamed at each other in the dim hallway. "We aren't sure she came up for that purpose," the wolf said. "But she refuses to explain why she was on the road."

"Perhaps she's a poacher," said John acidly.

"Sir," and here the wolf's professional law-and-order manner slipped slightly, "if you have another explanation for why a young lass from the village would be on the road to Tremontaine at four-fifteen in the morning, I'm sure we at the station would all be delighted to hear it."

"Well, what about our neighbours? The Barstows still live in The Kells, don't they? Or for that matter, the estate just outside the village? You pass the gate to Codder's Gardens before you come to Tremontaine."

"Yes, sir. The Barstows are away on holiday. They've left a polecat in charge of the house."

"Swanson, is it?" Mary said.

"Yes, ma'am. Swanson reports he never saw Miss Cooper, nor did he report any break-ins or thefts. As for Codder's Gardens, sir, the Harts live with their butler and housekeeper, and they too reported no visitors and no disturbances."

A pause, and then Mary said what Ellie and the rest of the staff were thinking. "It looks very bad against her."

"Constable Marston is searching the upper floor rooms again, but we did not find anything with her scent this morning."

"Of course not," John scoffed.

"Oh, Mr St. Clair," the wolf said. "That reminds me. Were you in the habit of borrowing your father's clothes?"

"It would be difficult for me to be in any 'habit,' Sergeant, as I've been home only two days. Three, now."

"Then you haven't taken a suit of his?"

"No."

"All right. It is likely nothing. Your mother thought he might have packed it in anticipation of a trip, but we have not yet found it."

Mary's voice: "How do you know one of his suits is missing?"

"Oh, as to that, well…" The wolf ruffled through his notes. "In our investigations of Miss Cooper in the village, two witnesses reported seeing Mr St. Clair in a double-breasted navy blue suit, but we were unable to find such a suit in his wardrobe."

"It's likely at the cleaners," John said tightly. "Or perhaps Miss Cooper has stolen it."

"We're searching her residence," the wolf said.

"I was joking, Sergeant."

"Murder is no joke."

"No, I know that—I just—"

"Sir, may I assure you that the Inspector is doing his very best to bring your father's murderer to justice?"

Flora murmured, "If he were doing his best, he'd have asked Donald about the suit."

The others hushed her, but while they listened for anything further from the drawing-room, Ellie squeezed Abby's paw. Flora's words had set off a train of thought, and if she were right, a lot of things might make sense. Unfortunately, if she were right, it would only look worse for Hope. But she was excited enough to want to know whether she was right, and if she could ingratiate herself with the police, it would make her feel better about lying to them.

The conversation in the drawing-room was coming to a close. Ellie let go of Abby's paw. "I'll come straight back," she said, and hurried back through the kitchen, ignoring the startled looks of the others.

The wolf in his police uniform was just walking slowly through the main room just outside the dining room, as she'd hoped. "Sergeant," she said, and he looked up. "I wonder if I might ask you one question."

"Of course." His eyes were tired and his ears out to the sides, but he gave her a long wolf's smile.

"You mentioned witnesses seeing Mr St. Clair with Hope. I wonder if any of them mentioned when they'd seen him there?"

"Oh, let me see." He flipped back through his pad. "Most recently, I think it was March twentieth."

"That was…" Ellie calculated in her head. "A Sunday, I believe? Didn't the Garden Society meet that day?"

"They may have." The wolf figured in his head. "Yes, that was a Sunday. Why?"

Ellie bit her lip and then leaned in close to the wolf. "At the base of the drive to Tremontaine is a gate-house. It isn't used anymore, but I believe if you search it, you will find Mr St. Clair's suit there."

His paw froze on his pad. He stared at her, eyes wide. "How did you know we were looking for Mr St. Clair's suit? How do you know it's there?"

"There are few secrets in this house, Sergeant." Ellie felt confident enough to give him a mischievous smile. "As for why the suit is there, well. I may be wrong. But I don't believe it makes sense for it to be anywhere else."

"Well, miss." He made a note in his pad. "We'll see soon enough. And if it is there, I might want to talk to you again."

"I won't be able to tell you much more," Ellie said, which was true. She wanted to talk to someone else first.

The sergeant eyed her. "Have you got any more duties tonight?"

"A few," she said. "Mostly cleaning up in the kitchen."

"Can your cook spare you? I'd like to walk with you to the gatehouse."

Ellie hadn't counted on this, but now she was trapped and couldn't easily say no. So she told Miss Turner she would be back in twenty minutes, and walked down the front drive of Tremontaine with the sergeant.

The evening had settled well, with only a purplish glow remaining of the daylight. Stars shone overhead as Ellie followed a half-step behind the wolf, watching his tail wag slowly. "Why do you think it's in the gatehouse?" he asked, once they were clear of the house.

Dry, cool grass gave way below Ellie's feet. She considered how to frame her response. "You know that Mr St. Clair enjoyed his… distractions," she said in a low voice.

"That appears to be a fundamental part of his character."

"I happen to know—please do not ask me how—that Mr St. Clair was…elsewhere, on Sunday afternoon of the Garden Society meeting."

"With a certain young lady, just not Miss Cooper?"

"Indeed." Ellie thought he probably assumed she was talking about herself, and she let him think that. "But if it was not him, it was someone who wanted people to think it was him. And then one assumes that this someone has played the part on more than one occasion. Therefore, the suit would be somewhere on the premises of Tremontaine where the person might change into it."

The wolf rubbed his muzzle, whiskers flicking like dashes of silver in the evening light. "Taken with his permission, you think?"

"I don't know." Ellie had wondered this as well. "I am not sure Mr St. Clair would have missed a suit."

They walked on in silence, around a curve of the drive, until the gatehouse came into view. "Did Mrs St. Clair know of Mr St. Clair's wanderings?" the wolf asked.

"I...don't know that, either," Ellie said. "I would have said no, but..."

"But?"

"I'm not married, sir," she said. "But I understand that husbands and wives often know things about each other that the other may not suspect is known." She stopped. "I'm not sure I said that properly."

"I understand what you mean." Cooke favoured her with a smile.

They had reached the small gatehouse, stone with a tiled roof. Despite being overgrown, the small cottage was in good repair. The wolf pulled a torch from his pocket and flicked it on, shining it on the ground. "Look there," he said.

The grass was bent aside in patches. "Someone's been here."

"Yes." The wolf held her back with a paw. "Let me go first, miss."

Ellie was sure there would be no danger, but she let the police sergeant walk carefully to the door, tail now curled against his side, both ears perked. He paused outside the door, then pulled it open with a quick motion.

Inside, he swept the beam of his torch across the walls. "Empty," he said, and Ellie hurried in after him.

She found him inspecting a worn brown suitcase. He tried the latch and it opened easily. Ellie held her breath as he pushed the lid of the suitcase up.

His torch shone on blue wool. "You are quite the clever weasel," he said softly.

Ellie's ears warmed and flattened at the compliment. The wolf bent down, bringing his nose right to the edge of the suit. Ellie could smell fox from where she was, but nothing more specific than that, and when the sergeant straightened, his expression was unreadable in the reflected light of the torch.

"Whose scent is it?"

He turned to her. Slowly, as though figuring things out in his head, he said, "Mrs St. Clair."

•

He walked her back up to the house quickly, swearing her to silence about the discovery. Ellie, at once flush with pride at her success and worried about what it meant, swore she would comply. She finished her duties, deflected Miss Turner's questions about what "that officer" wanted with her, and hurried up to her room to wait for Abby.

If anything, this new evidence weighed even more heavily against Hope. If she'd been having an affair with Mrs St. Clair, and Mr St. Clair had discovered it and threatened…what? Exposure, censure? Hope—and Mrs St. Clair herself—would have had motive to kill him.

Ellie didn't want to believe it was Mrs St. Clair. But if it had indeed been her husband's gun, if he'd been facing their bedrooms when he was shot…and yet something about it felt wrong to her. She puzzled over what it could be as she changed, but was still puzzling when Abby came back.

"Hullo, El," she said. "I heard you took a walk with a police wolf. Should I be jealous?"

"No, no." Ellie sat up. "I'm not bad at this detective business, it turns out. Only I feel like there's something I'm missing, something obvious."

"How can you be missing anything? It's the police have all the clues."

Not all of them, Ellie thought, watching Abby in the light of the oil lamp as the rabbit changed into her nightdress. "You said you wanted to talk to me about something?"

"Oh." Abby came over to Ellie's bed and snuggled up beside her, resting one paw on the weasel's stomach. The rabbit's ears drooped and she wouldn't meet Ellie's eyes. "I don't quite know how to say it. But I suppose I must."

When Abby didn't say anything for a good ten seconds afterwards, Ellie kissed the top of the rabbit's head. "What on Earth could it be, Ab?"

To her surprise, when Abby looked up, her brown eyes were damp with tears. "Oh, El," she said. "I thought you might have shot him."

"Me?" Ellie stared down.

"Don't hate me!" Abby gulped and then began to sob. "Only I saw you, I was looking out at the sunrise and I heard the shot and then saw you running off the terrace—I thought it was you. I thought there must be some reason for it only then you didn't tell anyone about it, and you looked guilty...and the more I thought about it, the more I thought you might have gotten fed up with how he, how he treated me, and, and..."

"Shhh."

"But El, I didn't think until later..."

"Shhhhh." Ellie pulled the rabbit against her. "It's only natural. But why didn't you tell me sooner?"

"When was there time? I was with the missus all morning, and then we just didn't have any time alone...but then I heard about Hope, and I realised that I probably saw *her* running off the terrace. It was dark still and I think I probably just assumed it was you."

Ellie took a breath. Abby shook in her arms. "You don't hate me, do you? I thought that you might have done it for me."

"The thing is," Ellie said. "The thing is...it *was* me you saw on the terrace. I think it must have been."

Abby stared. She whispered, "Then...did you...?"

"No!" Ellie hugged the rabbit. She spoke in a low voice. "I was out on the terrace watching the sunrise. I heard Mr St. Clair inside and then the shot, and then I ran off. And I didn't say anything about it to the police because I was afraid if the actual murderer knew I was there, he might come after me."

The rabbit gasped and held Ellie more tightly. "Oh, El! How terrible!"

"It would have been..."

"No, I mean—" Abby rubbed her paw up Ellie's side and rested her head on the weasel's shoulder. "You were right there! Right by him! How horrible must that be for you?"

"It was." Ellie exhaled. "It really was."

Abby tightened her arms around Ellie and nuzzled her gently. "And you've been carrying that around with you all day?"

"I got distracted trying to figure out who did it." Ellie told her a little about the detective work she'd done, and then had to boast about the walk to the gatehouse with the wolf.

"He sounds nice," Abby mused. "I don't think much of that Inspector, though."

"He's clever enough. He found out about Hope." Ellie stroked Abby's fur thoughtfully. "At first I thought there were too many people who would have wanted to shoot Mr St. Clair, and then I didn't think anyone had enough motive. Mr Trevayn, maybe, but the company is doing well and it sounds like he's going to be able to have his deal. Mister John—I shan't get used to calling him that—and Miss Mary both wanted to go off to school, but enough to shoot their father?" The weasel shook her head.

"Or Mrs St. Clair if she found out about Mr Giles and...I can't believe that just yesterday he was with me, and now..." Abby shivered, pushing the memory away. "Ellie, what if it was Mrs Kate? What would happen to us? If they sell Tremontaine..."

"Well, if they do...we'll find jobs nearby each other, that's certain." Ellie nuzzled the rabbit. "I won't abandon you."

"But we'll have to go and visit each other, and people will talk."

"Let them talk!"

Abby sighed and let her paw wander over Ellie's curves. "I wish I were strong like you."

"You're strong in a different way. You believe the best of people."

"You make it easy." Abby smiled up, one ear flopped over, and Ellie had to kiss her again, just had to. She couldn't resist that look. "It is funny about Mrs Kate, though. I never would have guessed!"

"She did hire both of us. Maybe she had a sense."

"It makes me feel a little better."

Ellie smiled down. "How much better?"

Abby kissed the weasel's cheek and moved her paw to the tie at the collar of the weasel's nightdress, picking at the laces. "Why don't I show you?"

•

It was a very nice night, and Ellie slept well afterwards with Abby by her side. She woke to Abby wriggling into her housemaid's uniform, in the pre-dawn chill of the room. Ellie pulled the blankets around herself and yawned.

Abby leaned down to kiss her. "I've got to go lay the fires, since Flora's down with Mrs St. Clair."

"I'll be down to start breakfast soon."

"Can I have a sweet roll?"

Ellie smiled back up at Abby's white face. "Another one, you mean?"

The rabbit laughed and kissed the weasel on the nose. "See you downstairs, dear."

Alone in the silent, dim room, Ellie felt a sense of optimism. There would be some changes, for sure, but the tension of yesterday, the nearness of Mr St. Clair's body (*don't think of it*), the fear for herself and for Abby—those things were fading below the routine of the everyday, the warm memory of Abby beside her, the compliment the wolf had paid her yesterday. She closed her eyes, and even though she knew she would have to get up in just thirty minutes, she drifted into a warm dream.

And then she heard Abby scream.

•

Ellie hurried down the stairs, still fastening her dress, propriety be damned. She burst into the main hall and found Flora holding Abby's shuddering form. "What happened?"

The otter gave Abby into Ellie's arms, and nodded toward the open door across the hall from them. "It's Mr Trevayn," she said in a low voice.

Abby drew breath and gave a louder sob. "He's dead!"

John came out, fastening a dressing gown around his waist, just in time to hear that last. "Who's dead?" He caught sight of the open door and walked to it, then into the study. A moment later, Ellie heard him exclaim, "Oh my God!"

He hurried out into the hall a moment later, ears flat against his head, tail curled down, eyes wide. "He's—" He looked at the three housemaids, and then another door down the hall opened, and his sister's muzzle poked out. "For God's sake, Mary, stay in your room. Someone call the police."

"I'll go," Flora said. She walked quickly down the main hallway, and then they heard her claws clicking on the stairs. She stopped to speak to someone.

Abby kept sobbing against Ellie. "I'd better take her upstairs," the weasel said to John. "You'll stay and make sure nobody interferes with the room?"

"What's happened?" Mary demanded, coming out into the hallway. "What's happened to Martin?"

She made for Mr Trevayn's room and John held her back forcibly. "Don't," he said. "For God's sake, Mary, listen to me!"

Her eyes met his. She struggled once more to get past him, and John was forced to push her back into her own room. "Stay there!" he ordered sharply, and pulled the door closed with a slam.

Mary pounded on it once and then was quiet. John stared at the door, ears flat back, and then turned to Ellie. "I'll watch the room," he said, just as Flora reappeared.

"Miss Kitt's up," the otter said. "She's calling."

Ellie, about to move Abby toward the stairs, realised that perhaps trusting John to secure the room was not the safest course. She met the otter's eyes. "Flora, you're not too tired to stay here?"

"No, no." Flora fluffed her whiskers up and smiled. "Quite chipper, actually. That little kip I had last night did a world of good. For now."

"Mother's all right then?" John asked in a low voice, looking down the hall.

"Sleeping soundly, last I saw her. I looked in when I heard Abby…"

"I'm sorry," Abby sobbed into Ellie's shoulder.

"Shh. Come on," Ellie said, and she left John and Flora to wait.

She didn't talk to Abby all the way up, despite her burning curiosity, but when she got Abby into bed, the rabbit clutched at her. "I keep seeing him, El," she whispered. "Laying out there like that."

Ellie bit her lip, her whiskers twitching. If Abby hadn't said anything, she would've just sat quietly and let her curiosity burn inside her. But now Ellie felt confident enough to whisper, "I didn't hear a shot."

"He wasn't shot," Abby said immediately. "Oh, he was lying on top of his sheets, without a stitch on, and his eyes were bugged out and his… his thing…" Abby covered her eyes.

Ellie gasped. "Was it…" She lowered her whisper even further. "Cut off?"

"No!" Abby shuddered again. "Good God, no. It was just…it was out, and purple…and his paws were tied…"

"Shh, shh." Ellie hugged her, feeling guilty. "Don't think about it."

"I can't not." The rabbit's ears lay back, her eyes squeezed tightly shut.

"Think of—think of the flowers in the garden, they're just blooming now. You like walking through the garden, right? And that dress Miss Mary was wearing, it was so pretty." Abby's breathing slowed. Ellie searched for more pleasant memories. "That meal we had, the purple carrots you liked so much…" She stopped as the rabbit whined and tensed. "No. Forget the carrots, remember the peas, they were so sweet and tender…"

After a few more minutes, Abby's breathing grew slow and regular. Ellie stayed there with a paw on the rabbit's chest as the sun brightened the room, bringing a soft glow to the white fur.

•

By the time Ellie went downstairs, the police had arrived. Inspector Bennett stood in the hall with John and Flora, while the wolf and constable were down the hall knocking on what she thought was Mrs St. Clair's door. The dawn had come, and Ellie could see the hall clearly, the badger's flat black and white face, John's sharp anger, Flora's whiskered worry.

"Now see here," John said, his tail bristled out, ears flat. "There are two witnesses—Ellie here will also testify—that I only came out of my room after the alarm had been raised. There's no reason to search it."

"Are you hiding something?" the inspector said in his ponderous voice.

"No—not at all—I just don't—you searched it yesterday, didn't you?"

"Then why should you object to us searching it again?"

"Oh!" John threw up his arms. His nostrils flared, and his whiskers spread. "Do what you must then."

"In the meantime, sir, may I ask your account of your actions last night?"

"Yes, certainly. I had dinner, spoke with your sergeant there, then walked my mother up to bed. I went to my room, read some newspapers and a novel, and fell asleep. I woke when I thought I heard a scream, but I—I was sleeping and I thought it might have been a dream until I heard people moving about out here."

Down the hall, the wolf was leading a sleepy Mrs St. Clair out of her room. The vixen held her dressing gown about her with one paw, her tail dragging on the floor. Flora ran to help her.

"You heard nothing in the night, then?"

"The usual. People getting up, moving about. Mr Trevayn left to use the necessary at one point, I suppose."

"The necessary?"

"Yes, Inspector." John's ears remained flat, his voice cold. "People have occasion to relieve themselves periodically during the day. It is a function of us living beings."

"Oh, I'm well acquainted with the various bodily functions," the Inspector said placidly. "Have to get up once or twice a night myself. The thing is, sir, Mr Trevayn had a necessary in his rooms. So he wouldn't have had to leave the room to use it."

"Then he left for some other reason. I heard the door, that's all I know. I told you, I was reading." His ears came up slightly. "When you can hear every little sound, you train yourself not to notice things so much."

"Ah, sir." The badger beamed. "That's where we're different, you and I."

The sergeant called out when he and Flora had helped Mrs St. Clair to the landing. "I'll just take the lady downstairs, shall I, sir?"

"Yes, please. In fact," the badger motioned to everyone in the hall, "why don't we all move downstairs. It'll be much more comfortable. You and the constable may start searching the rooms in a moment."

As they walked toward the stair, the inspector slowed his stride to keep pace with Ellie. "Miss Stone, I wonder if you might account for your actions since last night."

Ellie told him briefly where she had been, that she had spent the night with Abby until the rabbit had left to lay the fires. "And how much time elapsed between her leaving in the morning and the scream?"

"I was dozing," Ellie said, grateful to be able to tell the truth for once. "But perhaps half an hour? Sir, I'm sure Abby didn't do it. She was so horrified, and shaking."

"Yes. Well, once the passion of a crime has run its course, the murderer can often be overwhelmed by what he or she has done, you know. But in this case I am inclined to believe you. We have the coroner coming from Sherbourne, but I think he will find that Mr Trevayn has been dead for many hours. The body was quite cold."

"How...how was he killed?"

"Strangled," the inspector said. "And I am not sure that Miss Rose... nor you yourself, for that matter...would have the strength to restrain a powerful fellow like Trevayn. Although..." He stopped talking and stroked his chin as they made their way down the stairs.

Miss Kitt was pouring out tea for Mrs St. Clair and Sergeant Cooke. Nearby, Flora stood just inside the doorway to the kitchen, talking in a low voice to Miss Turner, otter and weasel hunched together. "I read about it in one of those papers," Flora was saying excitedly as Ellie and the inspector approached. "This fox in Japan, she and a rich bear took turns choking each other, said it was more exciting that way."

"So someone was in there with him?"

"Perhaps." Flora noticed the inspector and shut her wide muzzle. Miss Turner looked around and nodded.

But the inspector stopped too, and tilted his head. "Please, Miss Hayma, do go on."

"Oh," Flora said. "Only it went too far and," she whispered, "she killed him. Well, he died. I don't believe she meant to kill him."

"I see. Where did you read this?"

"It was in…" Flora's face scrunched up, trying to remember. "Some newspaper. I don't recall."

"A local newspaper? I don't recall the Sherbourne News having an international section."

"No." She looked pleadingly at Ellie.

"Oh," Ellie said. "Those were the ones in—" She remembered how agitated John had been, the bushy tail, the flattened ears.

The badger looked from the otter to the weasel. "Young Mr St. Clair reads the international news, I believe."

"Yes," Flora said in a low voice.

"But certainly there are many other people in this house who might have read those newspapers." The badger gestured to Flora. "Members of the household staff, for example."

"I never read nothing about that," Miss Turner said primly.

She would certainly have told Ellie if she had. "Or Mr Trevayn," Ellie said. "He might easily have done it to himself."

"He might at that," the inspector said. "It is a theory I am not discarding."

Behind them, Sergeant Cooke excused himself to join their group. "Good morning," he said, and indicated Ellie. "Sir, this is the weasel I was talking about who found Mr Giles' missing suit."

"Indeed." The badger smiled. "Excellent work, miss. Thank you for assisting the police."

"You're welcome," Ellie said, but felt a warm flush in her ears, remembering how she'd still not told them about being on the terrace. To cover, she burst out with, "Do you think the same person killed Mr St. Clair and Mr Trevayn?"

The badger and wolf looked at each other, and the inspector answered. "We have not yet developed a theory."

"Hope Cooper couldn't have done it, though, could she? She's been in custody since last night?"

"It would seem very unlikely," the badger agreed. There was a moment of silence. "All right, sergeant," the inspector continued. "Go on up and search the rooms, and I will talk with the residents of the house."

•

A short time later, a middle-aged fox arrived in a white coat, and the Inspector accompanied him upstairs as well. "That's the coroner," Miss Turner whispered.

"The ones in my novels are all foxes and wolves," Ellie murmured.

"Better senses of smell." Miss Turner tapped her nose.

"Blood all smells the same, I expect."

"They smell poisons that way."

"Oh, poisons." Flora waved a paw. "It's all very well in novels, but nobody actually poisons anyone, and if they do it's with rat poison, and you don't need to smell to know when someone's been poisoned with that. They certainly don't end up naked and…"

She paused just before Miss Turner said, "Hush," and looked around. Nobody else in the room was listening, though. The three foxes of the St. Clair family sat at one end of the room, talking in low tones, all their ears down. Mary seemed particularly affected by the events; she kept dabbing at reddened eyes with a handkerchief. Miss Kitt and Mr Pearson stood to one side as well, keeping to themselves, though the rat did exchange glances with Miss Turner from time to time.

"What if he was sleeping with someone in the house?" Miss Turner whispered. "Like…" She looked toward the three foxes, then at the deer and rat. "Miss Kitt, perhaps?"

"Oh, really," Flora said when Ellie didn't speak.

"Well, it wasn't one of us three," Miss Turner said. "Was it?"

"I was sitting all night in Mrs St. Clair's room."

"I was with Abby," Ellie said, "and it wasn't her, either. So Mrs St. Clair didn't go out?"

"No," Flora said, but slowly.

The two weasels looked at her. "Well," she said, "I did doze off a bit right at the beginning of the night, but it was only ten minutes or so. If she were going to go for to murder Mr Trevayn, she wouldn't be able to do it in ten minutes."

"And you might've woken while she were gone."

"How do you know it was only ten minutes?" Ellie wanted to know.

"She gave me a cup of tea," Flora said, "and had one herself, and it was just past ten. And then she went to bed and told me to be sure to wake her at seven for breakfast, and I remember looking at the clock and thinking, that's a good eight hours. So it was eleven. Then I sat down and closed my eyes for a minute and when I looked at the clock again it was eleven-fifteen." Her whiskers spread. "I remember because I was panicked, I thought I'd been asleep all night."

"Good job you weren't," Miss Turner said grimly. "So…there's Miss Mary."

"Her and Mr Trevayn? I don't see how that could be," Ellie said.

"He's been to the house before," Miss Turner pointed out. "And she's always been very cool toward him. Exactly as you'd expect if they were having a secret affair. Speaking of," she said before either Ellie or Flora could object, "I don't know that they'll let that Hope Cooper go. She could have shot Mr St. Clair, and then someone else killed Mr Trevayn."

"Miss Mary doesn't look like someone who just killed someone."

Flora and Miss Turner followed Ellie's gaze. "And why would she kill him if she were having an affair?" Flora said. "She could just marry him and have his money that way. Now it goes to his heirs, or his family."

"Maybe they're already secretly married," Miss Turner said.

"Then why would she kill him here?" Ellie shook her head. "It doesn't make sense."

The Inspector came back over to her, followed by Mary St. Clair. "Miss Stone," the badger said. "Would you please see if Miss White is feeling able to speak?"

"And then help Miss Turner in the kitchen," Mary said. The words seemed to come with effort. "I think we're all feeling a touch unnerved, and some breakfast would not come amiss."

•

Abby's ears still drooped, but she insisted she was able to talk to the police. She followed Ellie downstairs just in time to hear a loud argument in the main second floor hallway. "There isn't a gun in it, I promise you," John St. Clair was saying loudly. If he'd looked angry before, he looked fairly desperate now, eyes wide, ears plastered back to his head, his tone almost pleading.

Sergeant Cooke stood next to the constable, facing him. In the sheep's arms rested the wooden gun box. Beside the fox, the inspector leaned forward, and just around the corner on the stair, Ellie saw Miss Turner's pointed muzzle and Flora's blunt one peeking around.

In his slow voice, the Inspector said, "This was in your room the night before last as well?"

"Yes," John said, "but there's no gun, and anyway, you recovered the gun from the pond, didn't you? Please, just give it to me."

"The floorboards was loose," the constable said. "You must have put this back in a hurry this morning."

"I suppose I did." The fox turned from the sergeant to the inspector. "But Trevayn wasn't shot, was he?"

"Please, sir, this will all be unnecessary if you simply open the box," the sergeant said crisply, but still John lay his ears back and did not offer to help.

"Sergeant, you catch no scent of gunpowder?"

The wolf shook his head. "There's a scent of..." He paused. "It's curious. I don't recognise it. It's like petroleum jelly, perhaps?"

"Could it be gun oil?"

"I suppose it might."

"Sir." The Inspector touched his arm. "I hope you understand that if you do not provide the key, we will be obliged to force the box open."

"Oh, very well." John stalked into his room and returned with a small golden key, which he pushed into the inspector's waiting paw. His tail wound tightly between his legs and his ears remained flat against his head. "It's a fine day when the police can't take the word of someone who's done nothing wrong. I hope you won't mind if I don't stay to watch you humiliate me."

With that, he stalked down the hall, spun on his heel at the stair, and fairly ran down it. Ellie turned to Abby, and by mutual consent, they remained where they were. Abby's expression betrayed the same incomprehension that Ellie felt. If not a gun, then what *was* in the box?

That was the question now on everyone's mind. The Inspector turned to Sergeant Cooke. "I'll just take a short look inside to make sure there's nothing relevant to the murder," he said. "We can at least afford Mr St. Clair that bit of privacy."

He turned the key, and with care, lifted the lid of the box. His eyes widened. "I see."

At the same time, the wolf's nose flared, and he turned his head to look inside, then turned away with a cry and stepped back. The constable turned the box to see into it as well, and gave a shout of disgust. The box tumbled from his arms, and onto the carpet of the hall, fell—

"Oh!" Abby stared and then buried her face in Ellie's shoulder. The constable, staring at the ground, had recovered from his shock and was now braying with laughter. Ellie stared for a moment and then turned her head, the same as Abby was doing. She heard Mr Pearson's voice as the rat came hurrying down the hall, and then Flora asking what was going on as she ran up the stairs as well.

"Constable," the Inspector said evenly. "Please return Mr St. Clair's property to the box."

"I ain't touchin' those things," the constable said, with an eye at the sergeant, who was holding his nose. "Even I can smell where they been."

"Miss White," the Inspector said, and Abby turned. Ellie looked up too, trying to keep her gaze from the floor. "Would you be so kind as to fetch us some hand towels or handkerchiefs?"

"Yes, sir." Abby hurried into the lavatory down the hall and returned a moment later with three white squares.

By this time, Flora and Mr Pearson were gawking at the objects on the floor. The constable took the cloth from Flora and scooped them into the box, and when he closed the lid, all the eyes remained on it.

The Inspector coughed. "I trust we will be able to rely on your discretion. The character of Mr St. Clair is not on trial, and I am satisfied that the contents of this box do not relate to the murder of either Giles St. Clair or Martin Trevayn."

•

Ellie left Abby with the Inspector and walked downstairs with Flora. The otter barely managed to wait until they were on the staircase before erupting in excited, giggling half-sentences. "Oh God, Ellie, did you see—I can't believe our Master *John*—and does he put them *inside* him—he must, but both at *once?*—the white one was bigger than—well, let's just say I've never seen—not that I would know—did you have *any* idea?"

The weasel shook her head. She had not had any idea, but then, she hadn't known much about John at all. He'd been a quiet boy with eruptions of temper when he'd lived at Tremontaine, but he'd always treated the staff well. When he went away to school, his parents had thought he would come back for holidays, but apart from Christmas visits, he remained in America—making friends there, he said.

Flora had already skipped ahead to that speculation. "You s'pose he got those in America? Must have, I reckon. Can't think of a place even in Sherbourne—even in London—well, I suppose, London, must be you could get anything in London—but friends, I bet he had friends—that kind of people—oh, sorry, Ellie."

"It's all right."

"Boys are different, though, aren't they? Just seems…"

"It's all about what someone likes or doesn't like," Ellie said archly, "and I don't see why it would be all right for girls and not for boys." With that, she marched off to the kitchen to help Miss Turner finish preparing the breakfast.

Miss Turner, though fascinated by the contents of the gun box from John's room, was much more interested in the objects themselves than in the behaviour of young Mr St. Clair. "I suppose it wasn't *him* Hope Cooper was up here to see, then. But those things...well, I'm sure I don't know where he might have gotten one. Do you?"

Ellie shook her head. "I never." She watched the egg timer carefully.

"Much more fancy than what my friends had when we were young. It's no shame, you know. Why, one of my friends discovered something like that in the bedroom of a married lady, and her with a husband and everything."

"I've never even seen anything like them, I swear!"

"Speaking of," Miss Turner said, "isn't it terrible about Mr Trevayn? At least when Mr Giles went he was dressed up proper. Looked all dignified and sad, he did. But to go like that, all stretched out in his birthday suit and, well..." She made a clucking noise with her tongue. "It's a good job none of his family was around. It's bad enough young Mister St. Clair had his private...hobbies...exposed. Though he needn't worry about any of us talking in the village, I'm sure."

"Is there anyone in this house who'd like to have his or her private 'hobbies' exposed?" Ellie took the soft-boiled eggs from the saucepan and placed them gingerly in the cups. "Mrs St. Clair didn't have to go and dress up like her husband to meet Hope Cooper. Maybe Mr Trevayn really was just trying to choke himself. Abby saw a rope around his neck. And then there's me and Abby, you know."

"Oh, my dear, what you and Abby are doing, there's nothing wrong with that. I cooked for an old sheep who lived with a companion and yes, she had her own bedroom, but those bedrooms had connecting doors, and let me tell you, those doors did not stay closed. It's all about companionship, and you don't have families insisting you have a cub to inherit anything, so what's the harm?"

"Thank you. I think Abby is coming around to that thinking."

"She's young, dear. It's not easy. Speaking of, I do wonder about Miss Mary. If she were sneaking around with Mr Trevayn, well, pardon me for saying, but it's best that's come to an end. Perhaps she's one of those girls who's just waiting for a nice fox to sweep her off her feet. There was nothing wrong with that Mr Telcombe her father brought around."

"I liked Mr Channing better." Ellie set egg spoons on the plates with the eggs. "Is the toast ready?"

"Of course, you never know what they might have said to her in private. I imagine neither of them was keen on her attending university any more than her father was. Not that I understand that, but I suppose Miss Mary knows her mind well enough."

"She might have smelt something on them that we didn't," Ellie said. "How is the toast coming?"

Miss Turner allowed that this was possible. "Though weasels have good noses, too. It makes you a good cook if you can smell when the roast is done. I don't trust these modern gadgets."

"These modern gadgets pay your salary," Ellie said. Besides the refrigerator with the White Rose logo prominent on the front, the kitchen held an electric pot for boiling water and a 'toaster,' both of which stood cold and idle.

"That don't mean I have to use them." Miss Turner turned the toast rack over the flame and then removed it. She shook the toast free and arranged it on a plate. "Those things in that box—did one of them have a motor?"

Ellie coughed and raised her eyebrows as she took the toast. "Not that I could see. I've never heard of such a thing."

"Oh, well, you're young too." Miss Turner turned and gave Ellie a smug smile.

"You see," the weasel said with a glint in her eye, "there's another thing perhaps people wouldn't want talked about—"

"Yes, yes," Miss Turner said. "Speaking of, Miss Kitt says it's a light lunch, cucumber sandwiches and cheese, and we'll be serving the police as well."

"And the coroner?" Ellie didn't ask why the talk of motorised intimate objects brought Miss Kitt to mind.

"She didn't say." Miss Turner put a finger to her whiskers. "I suppose it depends on how long it takes him to determine cause of death."

"Cause of death," Ellie said. "The rope around his throat, you figure?"

"Could be." Miss Turner turned and whispered, "Did you see him?"

"No." Ellie shook her head. "Abby told me about him and that was as much as I wanted."

"Don't blame you." But the plump weasel sounded disappointed.

Flora and Abby came into the kitchen. Ellie lifted the tray to hand to Abby, but the rabbit shook her head. "Miss Kitt gave me the day off to rest," she said. "I'm going to lie down. Come up and see me if you get time."

Ellie smiled. "Rest up, then. Try to forget about it."

"I will." Abby smiled and squeezed the weasel's arm before going out the back hallway.

Flora helped load her tray. "I'm sorry about what I said, El. I'm just not myself, all this excitement, I swear, it reminds me of the war almost, in our apartment in the dark and the sirens going off and not knowing what might happen…I hardly know where I am from one moment to the next."

"It's all right," Ellie said. "I understand, I really do." She sent Flora back out to the dining room with a smile.

While the family ate, Ellie and Miss Turner talked in low voices in the kitchen. "Well," Miss Turner said, "I think Mr Trevayn did do it to himself. Celebrating his good fortune, if you ask me."

"Oh? What have you heard about the business?"

"Mr Pearson told me what he heard yesterday, and he was there when Mr Trevayn, God rest him, came back from his meeting." She paused. "Speaking of…I don't suppose you remember what Abby said about him?"

So Ellie dutifully recited what Abby had told her, enhancing some gruesome details she knew Miss Turner would appreciate. The cook oohed and aahed throughout, and then when Ellie'd finished, she continued her earlier story.

"So Mr Pearson says that Mr Trevayn looked pleased as punch with himself, but Mrs St. Clair, well, she heard what he did and she might have had ice on her whiskers after that."

"What did he do?"

"Held a meeting. It was scheduled for the morning, and Mr Giles was meant to go, but Mr Trevayn went himself in the afternoon. I suppose Mrs Kate thought it was disrespectful."

"So maybe," Ellie said softly, "someone killed Mr Giles to try to stop the meeting from happening, and then when Mr Trevayn went ahead with it anyway, they killed him too."

"Why not just shoot him?"

"Well, whoever it was had thrown the gun away." Ellie felt again the splash next to her in the lily pond. "Didn't have another one."

Miss Turner gave a most unladylike snicker. "Maybe they hoped to find a gun in Master—Mister John's box and got an unpleasant surprise."

"Miss Turner," Ellie said with some reproach, but couldn't hide a small smile.

"Honestly, it doesn't make any sense. Why take his clothes off and then strangle him?"

Ellie thought the Inspector had been asking that same question. "What if whoever it was convinced him to take his own clothes off?"

"And then sit there while she strangled him?"

"Abby said his wrists were tied too. Maybe he agreed to be tied up."

"Or asked to be."

Flora came back in just as Ellie was saying, "I never heard of that in any of the books I read."

"You should borrow some of mine." Miss Turner smiled at the otter. "How is the breakfast proceeding, dear?"

"Quiet," Flora said. "Nobody's talking. Master John isn't eating anything at all."

"Mister John," Ellie reminded her.

Flora went on as though she hadn't heard. "Mrs Kate just took her tea and egg and toast. And Miss Mary is still crying."

"Secret affair," Miss Turner said with smug satisfaction. "I told you."

Flora did not appear convinced. "Two deaths in a house would unnerve anyone."

"Perhaps. I'm only thankful Mr Pearson sleeps in the next room or I don't know how I'd get a wink at night."

"Well," Ellie said, "I rather think that the deaths were either from jealousy or for financial gain, and in either case I'm sure you've nothing to fear."

The plump weasel lifted her muzzle and fixed Ellie with a look. "For all you know, there might be many fellows interested in me."

"And would you want any fellow coming 'round to kill Mr Pearson?"

"Oh, don't even say it!" Miss Turner waved a paw. "For all we know, the killer might still be in the house."

•

Ellie and Miss Turner had just started the cucumbers for salad for lunch when the Sergeant Cooke pushed the kitchen door open. "Excuse me," the wolf said. "I wonder if I might borrow Miss Stone there for a moment."

The plump weasel raised her eyebrows in surprise. "He's in for a bit of a disappointment," she murmured.

"Miss Turner!"

The wolf coughed. "For some assistance in the case."

When she stepped out, she found the Inspector waiting.

"Oh, yes, she's quite clever. In that case, go, but don't keep her too long. We're preparing lunch."

"Of course not." The wolf turned to her. "Miss?"

He gestured to the servants' entrance, and Ellie followed him out.

To her surprise, when she stepped out into the soft spring morning, she found the Inspector standing with his paws clasped behind his back next to a large rosebush. "Here she is, sir," the wolf said.

"Ah, Miss Stone." The badger turned around. "Thank you for joining us. Following your insight yesterday, I wonder if you might have formed any theories after this last tragedy this morning. I have some, but it is always instructive to have the opinion of someone inside the house."

Ellie's eyes widened. She opened her mouth and closed it again. With the young wolf, she felt very much at ease, but the badger still seemed imposing even when he was being polite to her.

The wolf nudged her gently. "Go on," he said. "There's nothing to be afraid of."

"Well, sir," Ellie said. "It seemed there was some argument over the business. I don't know exactly what it was about. But Mr Trevayn and Mr St. Clair are both...are both gone, and what's to become of White Rose now? I gather there was a meeting, but I don't know what it was about."

Sergeant Cooke consulted his notes. "Mrs St. Clair told us that the meeting was to confirm the sale of White Rose Electrical to BOAC. The primary owners of White Rose—Mr St. Clair and Mr Trevayn—would have received payments that amounted to approximately two million and one million pounds." He flipped his pad closed. "Approximately."

Ellie looked from one to the other. "Am I allowed to know that?" she asked in a hushed voice.

"The articles of sale have been a matter of public record for some weeks. However," Inspector Bennett held up a finger. "Mrs St. Clair was opposed to the sale. She claims that she had convinced her husband to decline it."

"Decline two million pounds?" Ellie could barely conceive of such an amount of money.

Sergeant Cooke said, "She preferred to keep the company in family control. She says that the family did not want for money, and feared what might happen if a larger company took it over."

"I see."

The Inspector took over again. "However, we have no evidence that Mr St. Clair had actually agreed to decline the offer. He appeared to have dressed for the meeting, and Mr Trevayn insists that Mr St. Clair had every intention of completing the deal when he was shot." He leaned forward. "We would like to know if you, or anyone in the house, has any information one way or another about Mr St. Clair's intentions."

Ellie thought. "I haven't heard anything, sir, but I know he and his wife were arguing the day before—before he was shot."

The wolf and badger exchanged glances. "That appears to be in accord with what we know," the sergeant said.

Inspector Bennett nodded and stroked his whiskers. "In my profession, I am trained to see the patterns that underlie the confetti of details. When we cast aside the small details, we find the lines that connect intention to action. I believe that business had nothing to do with this. Mr St. Clair found out about his wife's affair, he confronted her—"

"Sir," Ellie said, breaking in boldly, "Mrs Kate takes a sleeping draught most nights."

"So she does," the badger said. "I meant, he confronted her that afternoon."

And maybe that explained why he had been so eager to take Abby, even though his wife was right below. Ellie frowned.

"We are still considering the possibility that Miss Cooper is involved, but it seems unlikely now."

She would have to ask Abby, unpleasant though it was, if he'd seemed…well, vengeful, perhaps, or simply desperate from having not had any opportunities in the past week.

If Abby could remember, and wasn't too upset by the question. But no, Abby was strong. Despite the shock of having her sometime-lover die, and then finding the body of the stoat…

That reminded her of something. "When I was cleaning his room," she said cautiously, "Mr Trevayn had a letter from a lawyer in his suitcase. It wasn't out on the desk with the other business papers. Do you know what that letter said?"

The Inspector, with an amused expression, turned to Cooke. "Sergeant?"

The wolf read from his notes. "It was a comprehensive—that means it was twelve pages long—treatment of the insurance policy around the company's primary officers which, according to the cover letter, had been updated with respect to the upcoming business negotiations."

"I see." Ellie didn't, but she felt comfortable with Cooke. "I wonder who it was requested the insurance policy be updated."

"Whoever it was, it was well timed," the inspector said. "If Miss Cooper did not kill Mr St. Clair, then we are left with the residents of the house."

"And Mr Trevayn?" Ellie could not help but notice that Sergeant Cooke stared down at his notepad during the Inspector's recitation.

"Assuming he did not strangle himself…"

The wolf coughed. "It would be most inconsiderate of him to do so while a guest, especially when his host and business partner had just been killed."

"Quite. As I said, if he did not strangle himself, then we are left with the question of who did. I would be inclined to treat Mrs St. Clair as a suspect—perhaps Mr Trevayn, who was awake at the time of the shot, saw something and had approached her with blackmail in mind."

And Ellie wondered, then, if Trevayn had seen her as well, if the purpose of his walk with her was to find out if she knew enough for him to blackmail her, or to enlist her help in blackmailing the killer.

"Speaking of Mr Trevayn, there is one more point that we might ask your assistance with," Sergeant Cooke said. "We understand he was given an extra-spicy dish at supper last night?"

"Oh." Ellie tried to suppress her smile. "That was Miss Turner's little joke. He had said her food was bland, so she added chilli sauce to his dish."

"Mm. And who else knew that she intended to add this sauce to his—potatoes, was it?"

"Oh, I suppose I did, and Flora bought it for her."

"Bought it? So you didn't have any in the kitchen?"

"Oh, no." Ellie shook her head. "You would know, sir. Canids can't abide over-spicy things."

"Quite." The wolf made a note. "That is what struck me as curious about it. So yourself, Miss Turner, and Flora knew that this condiment was to be added to his potatoes?"

"I didn't know what she'd put it in until after."

"But you knew it was going to something destined for Mr Trevayn. As, presumably, did Flora."

"Yes, sir."

"Sergeant," the inspector said, "Martin Trevayn was not poisoned."

"No, sir. But what if he were given a soporific, masked by the chilli sauce, so that when the killer did come to strangle him, he'd been made more docile?"

"A soporific. Like a sleeping-powder."

"Yes, sir."

The badger stroked his chin. "Well, we can ask the coroner to test for it. It will take a couple days, I shouldn't wonder. It's a good thought, Sergeant."

Ellie looked from one to the other. "You can't mean—you can't think—Flora?"

"We can't rule out anyone," the badger pronounced, and fixed her with a meaningful look. "The patterns may be suggestive, but they are by no means complete."

"But the good thing is that probably none of you are in danger," Sergeant Cooke said. "After all, the murderer killed Trevayn because he'd seen something. You and Donald are the only other ones who were awake, and you were both on the first floor."

Ellie's small ears flushed and flattened. They had put so much trust in her that she could no longer stomach having hidden something from them. That and the logic she'd put to Flora and Miss Turner, that there was no more danger, forced words from her. "Actually, sir," she said. "I have something to confess…"

•

They scolded her for lying, the inspector much angrier because she had "obscured his patterns," but they understood her fear. When she'd told them what she'd seen and heard, they looked at each other. "Seems to confirm that the shooter was not Miss Cooper, I suppose." The badger sighed. "Mr St. Clair knew the shooter well enough to recognise her—or him—in the dim dawn light."

"Or by scent," the wolf added.

"And the shooter knew there was a pond outside the window where the gun could be cleaned of scent and prints quickly. I had presumed that she—or he—ran through the garden and saw the pond as an opportunity. But if it was thrown from the window…"

"Accurately."

"Then it was someone familiar with the house and grounds, hardly a burglar." The inspector turned to the wolf. "Sergeant, I think we have enough evidence to release Miss Cooper. Please advise her that it will be in her best interest to be honest with the police about her activities at Tremontaine yesterday morning." He narrowed his eyes, looking at Ellie.

"I was scared," Ellie said.

"We won't tell anyone," the sergeant reassured her.

After that, they let her go back inside, where she ran into Miss Turner, nearly literally. "Oh, I was just coming to find you," the elder weasel said. "Cut the bread for the sandwiches while I prepare the cheese."

"Yes'm," Ellie said loudly, and then held a finger to her muzzle and set her ear gently to the door.

Over the hissing of the breeze, loud against the door, she heard the two officers talking. Inspector Bennett was dismissing the sergeant's suggestion, which must have been that Mrs St. Clair was responsible for both murders, on the grounds that Flora had been sitting in her room all night. Ellie nearly walked out to tell them about Flora's little nap, but two lies in one morning might be too much for them to take, and in any event it was Flora's lie to confess to. Then Inspector Bennett mentioned John's name.

"The son?" The sergeant sounded surprised.

"With what we know, we cannot eliminate the idea that Martin Trevayn might also have been a queer."

"Sir—"

"He's not married, is he? And that Mister Thorpe from BOAC, what did he say this morning? Something about Mr Trevayn 'going back to a lovely tail'? Well, what if that meant the son?"

"It needn't have meant anyone in the house."

"I feel it did, Sergeant." Ellie could almost see the inspector's black and white muzzle lift, the paw rubbing along his whiskers as he talked. "I feel it did. The patterns intersect here."

Their feet crunched on the gravel, and she hurried back to the kitchen, where Miss Turner demanded a review of everything that had been said outside, and then spent the half-hour prior to lunch spinning her own theories, while Ellie did the same in the privacy of her own head.

It seemed impossible that John would have killed his father, although if they had clashed over his homosexuality, then perhaps...well, at least she saw the fights he'd been in at school and the desire to run away to America in a new light. If she had the chance, she might go and talk to John—although his mother could do that as well, now.

But she still didn't see him as a killer. Of course, she couldn't really see anybody as a killer, so that made him as likely as anyone else, but Ellie felt a bond with Mrs Kate and with John now, and didn't want either of them to be guilty. In the case of Mrs St. Clair, it went beyond the commonality of their preferences.

Flora said it best when she came to the kitchen to prepare for lunch. "They're saying Mrs Kate is a suspect," she said. "With Mr Giles gone, what'll become of the house if Mrs Kate's arrested? We'll all be left without jobs. My sister worked for a red deer down near London, and he was arrested, and she and the whole staff were simply let go. No back pay, nothing."

Miss Turner wanted to know what he'd been arrested for, and Flora didn't remember exactly but thought it was something to do with theft from his company because everyone was being arrested for that these days, it was in all the papers, even in the American paper. "Of course, they're all criminals over there," she said. "If you read their paper it's all over theft this and murder that."

"And Japanese foxes strangling bears."

"Oh, that was in the International paper. But it's terrible. I'd never go to America myself."

"I would think it's much like England, with crime in the cities and not so much in the country," Ellie said. "There's all kinds of crime in London, but out here it's much more peaceful."

"Not here exactly," Miss Turner said darkly. "One more death and we'll all be looking for new positions, I shouldn't wonder, whether Mrs Kate is arrested or not."

"Oh, don't say that!" Flora shook her head.

"Surely Mister John would stay to manage the house?" Ellie said.

"Mr St. Clair," Flora informed them, "is having his things packed up and said he intends to go back to America."

Miss Turner laid down her knife. "He never."

"He is," Flora nodded. "He asked Donald to pack up, and Donald asked me for help, and I told him I had to serve lunch. Really." She leaned back against the wall. "He thinks I've nothing better to do."

"But Mister John," Ellie prompted.

"Oh, yes! He says they're already talking about his box down in the village, which I don't know about, but I suppose they will be soon enough. Everyone saw it, and anyone might have mentioned it to Johnny Brown when he came to pick up the milk bottles."

"Oh, Flora," Miss Turner sighed.

"It just slipped out." Flora fluffed her whiskers up. "Besides, he was bound to hear it from someone."

"Here, you take the sandwiches in. I'll have Ellie bring in the cheese."

"Me?" Ellie looked up, startled.

"Well, now Mr Trevayn's not there, there's no reason not to."

So Ellie followed Flora into the dining room and helped serve the cheese. The family were not at table, but instead standing around the parlour, so they placed the sandwiches and cheese on the side table and then walked about offering drinks to the foxes and the two policemen. The three St. Clairs all stood quietly, ears down, and spoke in low tones when they spoke at all. Sergeant Cooke and Inspector Bennett stood near them and the inspector made small talk, assuring the family that they hoped to have the investigation concluded soon. Ellie didn't miss the suspicious glances he shot in John's direction, but the young fox ate quietly and didn't say much at all.

The coroner came in and then hesitated when he saw the luncheon laid out. Inspector Bennett smoothed over the situation by inviting the white-coated fox to take some sandwiches, and then having a whispered conversation with him during which the fox gestured to the front door. Ellie heard only the end of the conversation, when the coroner said, "Two to three days, but I'll send the results along for sure."

"Was he killed?" Mary asked loudly.

The fox looked uncertainly at her, then at the inspector, who nodded. "In my opinion," the fox said, "the strangulation was performed with a pressure that is inconsistent with what Mr Trevayn could have managed on his own. That is simply a preliminary opinion—of course it is in the realm of possibility that he might have—but that is my initial opinion."

"So it's murder." Mary looked around the room and then set down her plate.

Silence reigned. The coroner glanced at the grandfather clock, which showed twenty to one, and cleared his throat. "I'd best be off. I told the station I'd be back by one."

"Is that clock right?" Flora squinted at the grandfather clock. "I thought it was earlier. I'm so bad with time these last days—"

"Flora." Mrs St. Clair's ears were up now, and she was looking right at the two of them. "Please run upstairs and fetch me the newspaper from my room."

The otter sighed. "Yes'm," she said, and set the carafe of water on the side table next to the trays of sandwiches.

"Mrs St. Clair," the inspector said, "I wonder if I might trouble you for a moment."

Mary and John moved slightly away from their mother. "Of course," the elder vixen said. Her ears flicked and she gave the badger a smile that did not, Ellie thought, have much warmth behind it. "We are anxious to help in whatever way possible."

"Sergeant Cooke and I would like to understand the disposition of Martin Trevayn's shares in White Rose, and whether the BOAC deal will still proceed."

"Oh." Mrs St. Clair's ears lowered, and her whiskers drooped. "I—I don't know. I confess I'd not given it any thought."

"You were upset with him yesterday."

"The deal—I felt it meant giving up on White Rose. I wanted to have something substantial to leave to our children. And Giles—it made Giles so happy to be running the company."

"But he was in favour of the deal."

"Until the day before yesterday." She pressed a napkin to her eyes. "Forgive me. I believe I had convinced him that he could build the company into something worth much more than two million pounds."

"To you."

"I beg your pardon?"

The inspector cleared his throat. "Two million to you. One million to Mr Trevayn."

"I see. Yes, I suppose that is right."

"And you have no idea who gets those shares now?"

Mrs St. Clair lifted her muzzle. "None whatsoever. I believe my husband said Mr Trevayn has a brother, but I really know very little about his family."

"He has a brother," Mary said clearly. "A younger brother, who lives in London. His father's passed, but his mother is alive and living in a small village in the north."

John and Mrs St. Clair stared at her. Mary laughed, showing all her sharp teeth. "Yes, I knew Martin. He was going to take me away, let me go to Oxford, like Father never would. Only I don't suppose that's going to happen now, is it?"

"Mary." Her mother moved toward her, but the younger vixen took a step back, the fur bristling up around her cheeks.

"Don't 'Mary' me, Mother. If I'd told you or Father, you'd have forbidden it. I know what you both thought of Martin. You thought him scheming. Father treated him like a servant. But he was more, he was clever and smart!"

Ellie had been looking at Mary's wide eyes and the fierce glow in them, and just behind her, John's jaw hung open and his right paw hung frozen halfway to clasping Mary's shoulder. Before he could complete the motion, Mary turned with a cry and ran from the room, her tail curled completely below the ruffle of her dress.

John took a step after her, but his mother reached out and held his arm.

"She's a foolish girl." Mrs St. Clair, like the rest of the room, seemed surprised at her own cold tone. She sighed and went on. "We spoiled her, gave her what she wanted, except for college. Giles—Giles thought that Oxford should never have admitted females, and for Mary to want to go there, well—it was the only thing they fought about." Her breath caught in her throat, and just as John, deprived of the chance to comfort his sister, put an arm around his mother's shoulder, Mrs St. Clair looked up with the same fire in her eyes Mary had shown. "If he'd known about her and that stoat, there would have been another fight," she nearly spat.

In the ensuing silence, Flora returned with a folded newspaper and held it out to Mrs St. Clair. "Your newspaper, ma'am."

"What?" the vixen snapped, and then stared down at the newspaper. "I don't want that. Throw it away."

"Mother, that's one of mine." John reached out and took it from the otter. He looked again toward the door where Mary had gone.

When Ellie looked back at the other side of the room, Inspector Bennett stood alone at the cheese tray, sniffing at a piece he'd just put onto a cracker. She hadn't seen the sergeant leave. But the tension in the room simmered enough that as Flora headed toward her with questions in her eyes, Ellie left and quickly walked toward the kitchen, taking plates and cups to wash up.

There, she washed while she told Flora and Miss Turner what had happened, and all the while she felt the feeling again, that there was something she ought to have noticed and hadn't. It wasn't about Mary and Mr Trevayn, although she thought that was important too. Not that Mary had killed her father, and she didn't think Mr Trevayn had killed him for Mary's sake, either.

"I never," Miss Turner said. "Miss Mary and Mr Trevayn indeed. Why, to think what might've gone on the nights he stayed here!" Ellie almost thought Miss Turner would like to have stationed herself outside the guest room door.

"You said you thought they were having a secret affair," Ellie pointed out.

"I don't want that. Throw it away."

"I never *believed* it," the cook replied tartly.

"So it was her he was talking to," Flora said, leaning against the door. "Using the house telephone."

"I don't know." Ellie thought about what she'd seen of Mr Trevayn's coolness, and Mary's passion. "*I* would say she was more in love with him than he with her. I expect all she meant to him was getting more power in the company."

"You can't know that," Miss Turner said. "Perhaps they were really in love."

"You never waited on Mr Trevayn, or saw them at dinner even." Flora folded her arms. "Neither of you. Nor heard him talking to her on the telephone."

"You did see them and you still didn't know about it," Ellie pointed out. "And he might have been talking to anyone on that telephone. Did you see that it was the house telephone?"

"I had inklings," the otter said. Her thick tail thumped against the pantry.

"You did not, or you would have told us." Miss Turner took a plate from Ellie to dry.

"I don't like to gossip," Flora said primly, which statement rendered Ellie and Miss Turner temporarily speechless. Flora took advantage of the silence to chatter on about a cousin of hers who'd taken up with an older gent and all was fine until she started to get a little grey around the muzzle and then one day she came home and there was a younger otter in her chair and a letter from the gent on her desk and that was that.

Ellie half-listened, and half-replayed the scene from lunch in her head, and then it came back, the thing she'd forgotten, and in that moment she saw with bright clarity the sequence of events.

"Ellie." Miss Turner was holding out her paw for the cup the younger weasel had just rinsed off. "Girl, what's the matter with you?"

"Oh." Ellie gave Miss Turner the cup and wet her lips. "I know who did it. I know who killed poor Mr Giles."

"What?" Flora said sharply, and Miss Turner held the cup so that it dripped onto the floor and made no move to dry it.

"At least," Ellie wiped her paws dry, "I think…well, I need to ask one question. Or, oh, perhaps I'd best have the sergeant ask it for me."

"Who?" Miss Turner demanded.

"The sergeant," Ellie said, distracted. "That young wolf."

"Who killed Mr Giles?" Flora had come over to stand next to Ellie.

"I shouldn't say until I'm sure. Oh, but I am fairly sure. But not completely." The weasel rubbed her whiskers. "What if I'm wrong? But I'm not."

Miss Turner took her by the shoulders, her bright eyes fixing Ellie's. "Who shot Mr Giles?"

Ellie took a breath and looked from the older weasel to the otter, both fairly hopping on the floor. "Well, I think—it must have been—Mr Trevayn."

Silence followed this observation. "Then he really was just celebrating?" Flora twisted her muzzle up. "Bloody bad luck."

"Watch your mouth, young lady," Miss Turner said.

"No," Ellie said. "No, I think someone killed him, too."

•

But after she left the kitchen through the back hallway and made her way to the drawing-room, she hesitated. The accusation would set off a chain of events, if she were right. It had been so clear in that moment of revelation, and now she was beset with doubt.

So she hurried upstairs to the third floor, and on her way up stopped to look out at the garden. Only two days ago she had looked out this very window and seen Mrs St. Clair working in the garden, and had thought it odd. Now Mr Trundle, the old mole, was back, shuffling around and trimming the bushes, and Mrs St. Clair was in the sun room coping with all the things that had happened over the last two days.

It occurred to Ellie that she had just behaved very much like the person in one of her novels who exclaimed that she knew something about the crime and then went off by herself and turned up dead before she could tell anyone what she knew. So she looked carefully around corners and listened and sniffed the air before walking quickly down to her room. If she were right, there was only one person she had to worry about, and probably not even that person.

But there was also only one person she wanted to talk to before she did anything, and that person was lying in her bed on the third floor bunched up in lilac-scented sheets and watching the clouds through their window.

If Ellie had a day off, she would lose herself in one of her police novels, or take a walk through the village, stop for tea and biscuits at one of the shops—with Abby if she were available—and probably poke her nose into Eldridge's to see what ingredients he had in that could make for interesting dishes, which was much different from going down to Eldridge's for specific things Miss Turner wanted.

Abby was content to sit up with her sewing and, Ellie saw, some old copies of Mrs St. Clair's "My Home" magazine. She picked one up as she sat down on the bed, and the rabbit turned to her with a smile.

"Afternoon, dear."

Ellie paged through the magazine. "Anything inspiring here?"

"Oh, there's a darling bedroom in this one." Abby tapped a thick claw on another magazine. "How is the house managing?"

"We all miss you." Ellie let the glossy colour pictures of other people's houses slide out of her paws, and leaned over to kiss Abby's nose, making it twitch.

"That's sweet." The rabbit's paw rested on Ellie's side. "Have the police gone yet?"

"Not yet."

A shadow flickered across those clear eyes. "I can't wait for things to get back to normal."

"I wanted to ask you about that," Ellie said.

"Me?" Abby sat up, brushing her ears out and cupping them forward, the black tips quivering. "Whatever for?"

"Well." Ellie twisted her paws together, and was silent.

Abby leaned into her and put an arm around her. "El, what is it?"

"Oh, Abby," Ellie sighed. "If someone hurt me—if someone did something to me—and you found out who it was, would you hurt them back?"

Wrinkles creased the rabbit's brow. "Who hurt you?"

"No, I mean." The weasel's paws fluttered. "*If.* Would you take it on yourself? Or would you go to the police?"

"I suppose—I suppose I would go to the police?" Abby brushed her lips to Ellie's cheek fur. "Is that what I should do?"

"What I mean is—" Ellie stopped. The words echoed in her head, but when she tried to say them, they sounded ridiculous. "If I know who killed Mr Trevayn, should I tell the police?"

Abby leaned back and sat up straight. "Ellie!" She searched the weasel's eyes and Ellie let her process that. "What a question. Why wouldn't you?"

"Because it might mean we couldn't be in the same house anymore. And because I don't think—that person—will do it again."

The rabbit's warm paws enfolded hers. "You think it was Mrs Kate."

The rabbit's warm paws enfolded hers.

When Abby said it, it sounded a little less ridiculous. Ellie nodded once, sharply. "But how?" Abby's brow lowered. "She was with Flora all night. And she took a sleeping powder. She could barely keep her eyes open this morning."

"Don't frown." Ellie squeezed the white paws back. "Flora said she dozed off. Only for ten minutes—she thought. But she only knew that because she'd looked at the clock in Mrs Kate's room. And she's been confused about time all day today. What if—what if Mrs Kate set her clock ahead, say, half an hour or even an hour, and gave Flora a sleeping-powder? Then she'd know Flora would be dead asleep for a while, and she could slip out. When she came back, she'd set the clock right and make a point of waking Flora up. And she was tired this morning because she'd taken her powder later than usual."

"I suppose." Abby shook her head, and looked down at the "My Home" magazines again, as though they might have etiquette tips on how to talk to your lover about murder theories. "But why would Mrs Kate do it?"

"Because Mr Trevayn shot Mr St. Clair. And she loved him. You told me that."

Abby nodded slowly. "She did, I think. They wouldn't have fought otherwise. I don't think she minded him being with me. It was just strange when she was here."

"But even then, she went out into the garden so she wouldn't be in the house. And the door to the shed was open when I looked out, and—" She was about to mention that Mr Trundle kept rope out in the shed, but hesitated because after that she would have to ask Abby if that had been the rope that had tied up Mr Trevayn, and Abby was in such a good humour that she didn't wish to spoil it.

Abby interrupted her reverie. "And you think he knew about her and Miss Cooper?"

Ellie thought she meant Mr Trevayn at first, and then realised they'd been talking about Mr Giles. She nodded. "I think it was an agreement between them. I think she found out sometime yesterday that Mr Trevayn had done it. Perhaps she suspected, because of the business. I saw her talking on the phone to someone…"

"What a horrible way to do it, though. Why not just shoot him?"

"I don't know. Well, he used Mr St. Clair's gun and then threw it away…and I suppose she saw that article in the newspaper, the one Flora was talking about…" Ellie rubbed her whiskers. "But what if I'm wrong? Or what if I'm right?"

"If you're right," Abby said slowly, "then you should tell the police."

"But…if I'm wrong, then I'll surely be dismissed. You can't accuse your employer of murder. And if I'm right, then…well, she only killed him out of love, for revenge. I mean, she's not going to turn around and poison half the village, is she? The inspector half-thinks Mr Trevayn did it to himself anyway, so…is it worth losing Tremontaine? Losing this room, being in the same house?"

"Mister John might stay—no?"

"He's packing to leave. He thinks his reputation won't allow him to remain here now. And Mary, well." Ellie told Abby briefly about Mary's bursting into tears at lunch. "I don't expect she will want to stay here either."

Abby looked down. "So we'd be separated, most likely."

"Most likely."

"It seems awfully selfish. Not to tell the police, I mean." Her eyebrows rose, and with them the black patch over her eye. A tentative smile curled the corners of her mouth. "I like that you're selfish for me."

"So you think I should."

"Well, you've told me now, El, so it's our decision together, isn't it?" Abby curled her lower lip under her front teeth and sucked gently. "Is there a way you could be more sure?"

"If the police could check for Mr Trevayn's fur or scent on the gun case—although Mrs Kate might have found it there too, or he might have used gloves—or, I don't know, I'm not a police officer."

The rabbit held Ellie's paws again, keeping them still. "Then ask a police officer."

Ellie stilled, took a breath, and kissed Abby. "Of course you're right, old soul. Thank you."

•

And still, when she went back downstairs to help set out biscuits for tea, she avoided Sergeant Cooke and the inspector. If someone had killed Abby, she thought, she would certainly burn to exact her revenge on that person. Never mind that she couldn't picture herself actually doing it. Mrs St. Clair was the lady of the house, and that afforded her an exceptional status, as far as Ellie thought. Not precisely above the law, but this fellow had murdered her husband in her house in cold blood—of that, Ellie was more sure than she was of Mrs St. Clair's guilt. It explained Mr Trevayn's walk outside with her. Of course, he'd been fishing to see if she'd seen him there, and he'd offered her the job to keep her close to him, beholden to him in exactly the way she was beholden now to Mrs Kate.

Miss Turner and Flora bothered her to tell them more, but she refused, even when Flora threatened to go and bring the sergeant around. "He's still here, him and that badger, poking around asking questions," she said, "and if you ask me, they'll be here longer than Mr St. Clair. He's called for a car to take him to London in the morning and he's shut up in his room. Miss Mary's shut up in hers, too. I don't know if either of them will be down to supper."

Ellie felt worse at that. Mrs Kate was now truly the only force holding Tremontaine together. She wondered if Hope Cooper would come to live here. Perhaps she was the 'help' Mrs St. Clair had in mind when she'd asked her husband if they could hire someone else.

Miss Turner, for her part, remained mostly silent as they prepared supper, and while Ellie was glad to lose herself in cooking, she found the lack of conversation unsettling. The clatter of pots and the smells of butter and roasting meat were not enough to occupy her, and again her mind swung this way and that without settling on any one resolution. But when she tried to initiate conversation, Miss Turner replied shortly, and Ellie knew she was being punished for her failure to share her thoughts.

And then came supper, and the busy bustle to get everything prepared. Of course it would be right in the middle of it, as Ellie was boiling potatoes, that Sergeant Cooke came back to the kitchen, nose twitching, his cap held in his paw.

"Smells delightful, Miss Turner," he said. "I wish we could stay."

The cook looked up, whiskers splayed. "You're not? But I made enough for five…"

Ellie hurried to the pantry, where she found a ceramic dish. "Here, Sergeant. We'll put some of it aside for you and the Inspector, and you can take it back with you."

"Oh, there's no need—"

"It's no trouble," Miss Turner said, taking the dish from Ellie. "And while you're waiting, maybe you'd like to ask Miss Stone if she has any more ideas about the murder this morning."

Ellie glared across the expanse of the kitchen, but Miss Turner bustled serenely about the stove, ignoring her.

"Miss Stone?" The wolf stepped forward. "Would you like to talk outside?"

"Oh, you can talk to her in here," Miss Turner said. "I don't mind at all."

In the following silence, the sergeant cleared his throat. "I could wait out in the drawing-room."

"Miss Stone thinks Mr Trevayn killed Mr Giles," the plump weasel said without taking her attention away from the hob and the mushrooms she was pushing around the sizzling pan.

Ellie poured out the boiling water into a colander, breathing in the potato-scented steam. When she lifted the colander to the sideboard and finally turned to the sergeant, she saw that the wolf's eyebrows were raised, his ears perked. "And why is that?" he asked politely.

She exhaled, blowing steam across the room, and wiped moisture from her whiskers and muzzle. "For one million pounds," she said.

"I mean, why do you think that? What evidence do you have?"

"I haven't any evidence," she admitted. "But Mr Trevayn was snooping around the day before, and I think he saw Mr Giles…" She coughed delicately. "With Abby—Miss White, I mean. And that morning, when I heard Mr Giles…well, I didn't realise it at the time, but he said, 'Oh, there you are,' and I thought he was talking to me."

The sergeant's ears flicked. He nodded slowly. "It was the way he said it, you see," Ellie said, talking faster. Her own ears flushed. "It was the way he would talk to a servant. And it was someone he expected to see. So it might have been me, because I was laying the fires, or it might have been Flora, who usually lays the fires, or it might have been Donald, who was supposed to be getting the car ready." The words came in a rush now. "But Flora was asleep, and Donald was out front, and I was on the terrace. But there was someone else he talked down to, as if they were a servant."

"Martin Trevayn."

"Yes. Me, or Flora, we don't mind. We're hired help, and he may talk to us that way if he likes. But I think for Mr Trevayn, it rankled him. He was courting Miss Mary, you heard."

"Yes." The wolf bared his teeth for a moment. "Not because he loved her, you think."

"I would be very much surprised," Ellie said. "And I think—and so does Mrs St. Clair—that Mr Giles had decided at the last moment not to sell the company. And so Mr Trevayn saw his one million pounds going away like…" She waved at the steam still rising from the potatoes. "Like steam. And that was possibly the last straw for him."

The sergeant stroked his muzzle thoughtfully. "It's plausible. If he needed the money quickly, say. How tragic, though. Murders his business partner and then dies… 'celebrating.'"

He looked keenly at Ellie, and though the young weasel stayed silent, her superior did not. "She don't think he died naturally, either."

"I could be mistaken about that," Ellie said hurriedly. "It's much less—I mean, it's instinct."

"I tend to agree," Sergeant Cooke said, his tail swinging back and forth. "It's not specifically out of character, but, you know." He sighed and rubbed a paw across his ears. "Difficult to say what a fellow does in his own private time. I mean, who would've thought that Mr St. Clair the younger…well, at least Martin Trevayn never went to America. Nor Japan."

"Maybe he wanted to try exotic things." Miss Turner sounded as though she held a lingering grudge about the dead stoat's comments, unleavened by his demise. She tipped the mushrooms into a bowl and pointed at the sideboard. "Melt some butter on those, and then parsley."

"What does your instinct say?" The wolf's eyes caught Ellie's.

"I don't like to say." She shifted, broke away from his gaze, and reached to the refrigerator for butter. "What if I'm wrong?"

"What if you're not?"

She rubbed her whiskers back and let the cool air of the refrigerator wash over her before closing the door and carving off chunks of butter. "I don't like to ruin someone's life simply on account of my instinct." Moving to the stove, she said, "I witnessed a murder. Perhaps I have murder on my mind."

The wolf grinned, coming to stand next to her as she melted the butter. "You seem like a very steady, stable young lady. We won't make any arrests simply on the strength of your instinct, but I would trust it."

"That's very nice," Ellie said, as Miss Turner made a great deal of noise bustling around pots and pans, scooping meat and potatoes into the ceramic dish. "But I'm not certain I do. Not yet."

"All right. Well, ring us up if you become more certain."

"Wait!" She kept an ear tuned to the sizzle of butter melting as she faced him. "Does the inspector have a suspect?"

"Oh, who can say?" The wolf paused for a moment. "The Inspector has his own methods, and they may look hodgepodge to some of us, but he gets results."

The cant of his ears gave Ellie a clue about what he thought about those results, but she hid her smile and returned a serious nod. "I will be interested to hear his thoughts," she said.

"I can tell you that right now he does not suspect any of the staff. I will of course come and see you if his scope narrows to one person." He paused, and now his ears tilted again, but with a silly half-smile on his muzzle. "If I might, that is."

"Of course," Ellie said.

Miss Turner pushed her bulk between the two of them, holding out the dish to the sergeant. "You come and see her any time you like," she said. "I can spare her for a small talk with such a handsome sergeant. Ellie, drip some butter on the sergeant's potatoes."

Sergeant Cooke bowed to her as Ellie lifted the pan and poured butter over the small mound of potatoes in the dish. Miss Turner sprinkled parsley on them and then placed the cover on it. She told him to bring the dish back tomorrow, and he told her he hoped he would be able to resist eating before they got back to the station because it smelled so delicious.

When he was gone, Ellie swatted Miss Turner on the arm. "What was that about? 'You can come and see her any time'?"

"Well, dear, it's all well and good what you and Abby do, but someday you'll have to get married, won't you? He's a good fellow, makes a decent living, and nobody'll expect you to have cubs."

"I'm not looking to get married," Ellie said.

Miss Turner smiled. "You're young. Give it some time. Now wash those greens and let's get supper on the table."

•

In the bustle of supper, Ellie was able to push her suspicions away from her mind and lose herself in the welcome routine of serving. She helped Flora bring the food out to the table, which she'd missed during the days Mr Trevayn had been there. She liked seeing the foxes breathe in the first scent of dinner, seeing the smiles spread over their muzzles— though tonight, smiles were in short supply.

At least Mrs Kate had convinced her children to come down. John kept his ears down, hunched over his plate as though contained in a private bubble, his tail curled tightly under his chair. Mary kept rubbing at her eyes and staring at her plate for seconds on end without moving. And Mrs St. Clair herself ate slowly, looking across the table at the empty spot where her husband would normally have sat. Ellie watched her for signs that her theory was right, but she couldn't tell whether the weight that lay on the older vixen's shoulders was guilt or simply sadness at losing her husband.

"It's very nice," Mrs St. Clair said when she looked up and saw Ellie. "Please tell Miss Turner I shan't want pudding."

"Nor I," said Mary in a thick voice.

John said, "I'll be leaving in the morning."

"I wish you'd stay," Mrs St. Clair said, but Ellie thought she sounded tired, pleading because it was a mother's duty.

"For what?" John threw his fork down on the table. "To be looked at and mocked every time I step outside the house? Even inside it?" He glared at Ellie then, and she looked away, retreating a step toward the kitchen.

Flora, standing next to her, showed no signs of wanting to leave the room. Mrs St. Clair opened her muzzle to say something, and then looked at Ellie and Flora. "Has any of the staff said anything to you?"

The younger fox didn't look up. "I'm sure they're talking about me."

"Where will you go?"

"I've rung up Charlie Patterson in London. He says I can stay with him for a few days. I'll wire some friends of mine in New York. I can find a place, maybe finish school."

His mother ate mechanically. "Your father would have wanted you to look after White Rose."

"He's not here, is he, mother?"

She laid down her fork and looked levelly at him. "No, John, he's not."

He met her gaze and then dropped his head. "I'm sorry."

"Yes," she said. "So am I."

That was the entirety of the conversation over supper. Ellie helped Flora clear the table of plates, and she and Miss Turner did the washing-up while Flora served tea and then came back to the kitchen to talk to the weasels.

"How's Abby?" she asked, and Ellie told her that Abby was doing well and did not seem to have any lasting effects of having found Mr Trevayn's body. "That's good," Flora said. "They're all still glum in there, between Mr St. Clair dying and Mister John leaving and Miss Mary—well, I had no idea! Nor had any of us, I suppose. You think she might have had something to do with it? He was," she lowered her voice, "naked, you know, and maybe she was doing something, and it went wrong, you figure? I don't know. I never would think to do nothing like that."

"It was his idea if she did," Miss Turner said.

"You don't think it was Master John, do you?" Flora said, and Ellie, tired of correcting her address of the new Mr St. Clair, did not interrupt.

"I reckon I wouldn't put it past Mr Trevayn to cheat on Miss Mary, but it don't seem like Master John. Then again, he did have that newspaper with the bit about the Japanese fox in it…though I did read it in Mrs Kate's room. And Master John is awfully keen to be on his way. Does he get the money from his father or does Mrs Kate have it all?"

Nobody knew the answer to this. "Oh well," Flora chattered on, "they're all in a right state. I told Mrs Kate her tea was bitter and she snapped at me. Miss Mary won't say a word, and every time I look at Master John he jumps like I'm accusing him of something."

"Terrible tragedy," Miss Turner said. "We just have to keep the house running and let them get past it. Mrs Kate will keep the house together."

Ellie dragged a cloth across a dirty plate, and she wondered about that. She couldn't stop seeing poor dead Mr Giles in her head, but that image did nothing to help her decision. Someone who could kill another person, could snuff out a life, they deserved to be punished, did they not? But what if the person who had been killed had also taken a life? Martin Trevayn had a family, people who loved him as much as Mrs Kate had loved Mr Giles, and those people would be grieving just as much. But Mr Trevayn had been the one to shoot Mr Giles.

Her novels were no help. There was little grief in them; when someone discovered the murderer, he or she reported it immediately—or else was killed before they could. She didn't think she was in any danger of being killed, but neither could she bring herself to end her tenure at Tremontaine by accusing Mrs St. Clair. In the end, she couldn't trust herself to make any choice, which was itself a choice.

•

She and Abby rested together in bed, the evening clouds dark violet outside their window. Abby's paw rested on Ellie's stomach just below her breasts, and Ellie's arm supported the rabbit's shoulders. "Did you decide?" Abby asked, after many minutes of comfortable silence.

Ellie, who had been thinking about Miss Turner's comments, started and then nuzzled the rabbit's long ear, which lay next to her muzzle. "Not entirely yet."

"But you didn't tell the police." Ellie shook her head, and Abby settled against her. "Well, whatever you decide I'm sure is best. I think murder is terrible, but if he was a murderer too, then maybe it's not so terrible?" She exhaled across Ellie's fur. "If someone killed you, I'd want to hurt them, I suppose."

The weasel tightened her grip on Abby's shoulder. "I wouldn't want you to. You shouldn't have that on your conscience."

"But Mrs Kate can have it on hers?"

"Nothing I do will change that. The question is whether she should be punished for it." Ellie paused. "If she even did it. I can't prove it at all."

"It's not your job to prove it," Abby said. "It's the police's job."

"I just don't know." Ellie exhaled, and Abby rubbed her nightdress gently, smoothing the fur below.

Their door opened, and Flora came in. The cup of tea in her paw rattled on its saucer as she stopped short. "Oh, wrong room again." She shut the door behind her. "Silly me. Sorry, won't be a moment."

She sipped the tea and twisted up her muzzle. "She said I should try it again, but it's just as bitter as it was last night. More, if anything." She walked over to Abby. "Here, try it."

"Flora," Ellie said, as Abby sipped at the tea, "did you wake up on your own last night? From your nap, I mean."

"Who else would have woken me?" Flora said. "Though it's funny you should mention. I believe I heard a door close and that might have jolted me awake. But when I checked on Mrs Kate, she was asleep." She rolled her head from side to side. "I know it was only fifteen minutes but my neck was stiff and I felt terrible for having gone to sleep. It's funny, I had a short nap this morning and now I barely feel tired at all. Usually I don't sleep sitting up in a chair, I suppose. But it's a little odd all the same. Like that business with the clock."

"You're right." Abby gave the teacup back to the otter. "It does taste rather bitter. Is that how Earl Grey is meant to taste?"

"What business with the clock?" Ellie sat up a little straighter.

"Oh, it's just me." Flora took the teacup back and sipped, and grimaced. "I thought it was just going on ten o'clock, but I must have been distracted, because then I was escorting Mrs Kate to bed and it's all of a sudden going on eleven."

"Did she offer you tea when you went up?"

Flora squinted. "Now how would you know that? Oh, because I just told you I had it last night." The frown relaxed into her familiar smile. "I swear, sometimes I can't even remember what I've been saying from one moment to the next. It's a wonder I don't lose more hours here and there." She sipped at the tea and yawned. "I'm proper tired now. Goodnight, ladies. I'll see you in the morning."

She disappeared through the bathroom, where they heard her run the water before retiring to her bed. "She's sweet," Abby said. "The thing you were asking about the tea, that was about Mrs Kate giving her a sleeping-powder, wasn't it?"

"Yes," Ellie said, and then looked down at the rabbit, her skin prickling with a fear she didn't want to allow full rein to. "How bitter was the tea?"

"Oh, I don't usually drink the Earl Grey," Abby said.

"No, none of us do." Ellie squeezed the rabbit. "Was it bitter?"

"Rather. I don't know why she keeps drinking it."

Ellie sat with her back against the pillow, and her heart pounded in her chest. Abby's expression turned from curious to concerned. "Dear?"

In a quick movement, Ellie threw the covers back and scrambled across Abby. "Stay there," she said, "and if you start to feel sick, come to the bathroom." Before the rabbit could answer, Ellie had hurried through the cold white porcelain of the bathroom.

Flora sat on the edge of her bed, teacup in one paw, her muzzle twisted up against the bitterness. She looked up at Ellie with surprise and opened her mouth, but Ellie cut her off.

"Stop drinking that!" She amazed herself with the command in her voice.

The otter, too, was taken aback. She lowered the cup to the table and then stifled a yawn, looking up at Ellie. "It's nearly gone anyway."

The cup was a third full, maybe a quarter. "Oh, dear," Ellie said. "Don't touch it. Don't throw it out. Oh, my God, I hope I'm wrong."

"Wrong about what?" Flora yawned again, and her eyes drifted closed. She lay back in her bed. "I'm sorry, El. Last night is catching up to me all at once."

"No, it's not." Ellie grabbed the otter's paw and pulled her toward the bathroom. Flora was heavily built and difficult to move. "Come on, Flora!"

"Oh, let me sleep." Flora twisted her paw out of the weasel's grip.

"Flora!" Ellie stood there for a moment staring at the prone otter, and then came to a decision. "Abby! Are you awake still?"

"Yes." The rabbit appeared in the doorway. "What's going on?"

"I think there was sleeping-powder in the tea. A lot of it." She pointed at the teacup. "Don't let that out of your sight and don't let anyone pour it out. I'm going to fetch some ipecac from the downstairs. We've got to make her sick."

"You're talking nonsense," Flora murmured, but her voice wavered.

Abby stared at Ellie. "I can't," she murmured.

Ellie squeezed the rabbit's paw. "Just watch over her. I'll be right back."

•

"It's good you called us when you did," Sergeant Cooke said to Ellie. His tail wagged slowly.

They stood at the front door of Tremontaine. The doctor had just come down to tell them that he'd administered a stimulant to Flora and expected her to be fine. The constable was inside securing the house, and the cup of tea was in the police car waiting to be analysed.

"Abby drank some of that tea." Ellie couldn't get that image out of her head.

"Calm down." The wolf reached out to hold her arm. "At worst, there's likely just sleeping powder in it. She was tired from a long day and a night when she didn't sleep much, so there may have been nothing. And Abby—Miss White—isn't showing any signs of distress. She's tired, that's all."

"I should have told you before." His touch was calming, but Ellie wanted her white rabbit, wanted to know for sure that Abby was all right. "I didn't realise how scared I would be. She might have poisoned Flora, or Abby."

"Or you. But listen, can you do something for me? Are you calm enough? We don't have much time." He looked into the house.

"I think so." Ellie turned her ears to him.

He leaned in and told her, in a few short sentences, what he wanted her to do. "Can you do that?"

"Yes." Ellie nodded once, a movement much more decisive than she felt.

"Good—here she comes." His ears perked. "I hope we're right about the angle to take."

Mrs St. Clair, looking elegant even in a white dressing gown, swept out from the parlour where Flora was resting. Her black ears were up and her tail curled gracefully behind her as she came to stand next to the sergeant. "I am told that Flora will survive the night," she said with a slight sarcastic edge. "Now, can someone tell me exactly why the doctor was called? Was Flora ill?"

Ellie started to reply, but the sergeant squeezed her arm. "Miss Stone here tried to wake her and found her unresponsive," he said. "She thought—quite reasonably, if you ask me—that after a shooting and a strangling, anything odd ought be reported to the police. I took the call and brought the doctor up to be safe. I'm pleased to hear that Miss Hayma will recover."

The vixen turned to Ellie. "You thought Flora was *poisoned*? By whom, exactly?"

Ellie took a breath. "By whomever killed Mr Trevayn."

"And Giles, no doubt."

"No," Sergeant Cooke put in. "We know Martin Trevayn killed Mr St. Clair."

The vixen's eyes widened, and her ears perked. "Oh, you *know* that, do you? Well, then, who killed Martin Trevayn?"

Her nostrils flared, and her breathing came quick and fast. She was tall enough to look the sergeant in the eye, but he didn't shrink from her gaze. "You did, ma'am."

She froze. Ellie saw the truth in her eyes before she laughed, harshly. "I did, did I? Well, I won't say I wouldn't have liked to, but I'm afraid you'll find that difficult to prove."

"We have a few of your hairs from Mr Trevayn's bed."

She flinched, but did not look away from him. "Indeed. I checked the guest room thoroughly before Mr Trevayn's arrival."

"And we have Miss Stone's testimony."

The vixen's icy eyes fixed Ellie. "Really. What has Miss Stone been saying?"

Ellie swallowed, but thank the Lord, the sergeant kept talking for her. "It was something she hadn't thought important enough to mention right away."

"Not until Abby said something about the rope." Ellie improvised, hoping it would be okay. "I didn't see it, but she said something about Mr Trevayn getting the rope from the garden shed."

Mrs St. Clair kept her demeanour cool and composed, her ears upright, whiskers immobile. "He might have. Anyone might have."

"But..." Ellie said the next words with all her heart. "Forgive me, ma'am, but I saw you carrying it back, from the second floor window."

The vixen stared, and then laughed. "Ridiculous," she said. "You're lying."

"I'm not." Ellie couldn't keep her own whiskers from flicking about.

"You are. You were in the kitchen when—"

Her eyes widened, realizing her mistake a moment too late. "When was this meant to have happened?" she asked, but it was too late and she knew it as well as Ellie and the sergeant did.

"Mrs St. Clair," the wolf said, his voice soft, "I have enough evidence to arrest you. I have enough evidence to bring before a court. You may be correct—we may not have enough to convict. I'm not a barrister. But the scandal, the expense—think of the strain on your family! If you confess, well—I believe we can paint it as a crime of passion. Who would not sympathise? This man shot your husband and continued to live in your house! I am sure you can tell us a story, that he invited you to his room with promises, perhaps, of letting you retain control of part of the company; that you, ashamed, arranged for your maid to be asleep for an hour; that he had read of this Japanese fox and wanted you to choke him; how the anger overwhelmed you and you could not stop." His eyes held hers. "And, of course, how terrified you felt afterwards, fled the room, returned to your bed and tried to forget it all."

The vixen did not answer. She stared back at the sergeant. "It will all be over quickly," he said. "The details of the case need not ever be reported, only that you strangled him. You will serve perhaps ten, twelve years. Everyone will speak of you as a brave widow—if you confess, if you do not fight. You can set the terms of your punishment. And your children will be—"

"Ha!" She barked, a sound that made Ellie jump. "John is running off to America to be queer, and Mary—Mary will never forgive me."

"As to that," the sergeant said. "I think we can help. Mr Trevayn kept a girlfriend in London, did you know that? A stoat with rather expensive tastes. He'd promised to marry her when the deal was complete."

She stared at him. "Then why—why was he courting Mary?"

"Because," Ellie said, working it out in her head, "he thought she might be useful leverage on Mr St. Clair. She used to talk to him about the company, didn't she? She got him to invite Mr Trevayn here. There was no real reason they couldn't have met in the city." Of course, that afternoon on the telephone, he hadn't been talking to Mary on the *house* phone. He could have just gone up to see her. He'd been talking to his other girl.

"Yes." Mrs St. Clair appeared dazed. "That—swine." Her fists tightened, and Ellie wondered if she were reliving the moment in which she'd choked him. "Whoever—whoever killed him deserves a medal, not a trial."

"Public opinion will undoubtedly be on your side," the wolf said gently. "But I represent the law, and the murderer of Mr Trevayn must be brought to justice. I am certain a sympathetic jury will find for a short sentence."

And if Mrs St. Clair confessed, then Ellie didn't have to perjure herself on the witness stand. The weasel watched her employer and saw her resolve melt away, the sag of her shoulders as she accepted her fate.

"I never liked him. He pushed Giles to make this deal, to sell the company he'd worked so hard to build. I didn't like the deal. I didn't think we needed money now. What legacy would that leave for our children? White Rose had the potential to be much more, to grow and flourish, and they were going to throw it away the moment someone waved a pile of money at them."

It was easy to be so casual about two million pounds, Ellie thought, if you'd always grown up with money.

"And then poor Giles—I loved my husband, Sergeant, though you may not believe that. We no longer shared certain things, but we had agreements and we shared a life, still. I was certain he'd been murdered for the money, and when I found out that Martin Trevayn had called to postpone the meeting before Miss Kitt had even notified the police of the murder, well, I was sure of it. I smelled him on the gun case."

"Why didn't you tell the police?"

"And then what? An investigation, possibly an arrest? White Rose sold and portioned off before anything could be done? No. He strutted about the house like a little popinjay, so proud of himself. Well, I called the BOAC people and the White Rose board and I found out what he'd been doing—asking around, ensuring he would have control of the company if anything happened to Giles, that he could still put the deal through. He'd been planning this for a month."

"You have proof of this?"

Her fangs showed over tightened lips. "I heard his confession before he died. Do you count that as proof?"

"Given that you killed him just after, I have to say that any court would find it suspect."

Ellie lowered her eyes. She did not think she would be able to kill someone, even someone who had killed Abby. But nor did she think she would have the strength to feign interest in Abby's killer long enough to get him tied up and at her mercy in the first place.

"I should have found a witness." She exhaled. "I will pass over the rest of the story, if it's all the same to you. Thank God I didn't know about

Mary then, or I might not have been able to get him to my advantage as I did. *He* was eager enough to have me, the filth. Let him be remembered as a murderer."

"I think we can manage that," the wolf said. "We have enough evidence to make a case against him. Thanks to Miss Hayma, we all know about that Japanese bear."

"Yes. Flora did talk about that article, as I'd thought. Only she wouldn't stop talking about the time." Mrs St. Clair shook her head and met Ellie's eyes, with a severe frown. "But I did not poison her. And I am disappointed that you would think that of me, Ellie."

"I'm sorry, ma'am," she said. "I was scared."

"Well. I hope your mind is at rest now."

It wasn't, but Ellie had a moment to think over the problem while the Sergeant took Mrs St. Clair to the constable and gave him instructions. By the time the wolf returned, the cool night air had cleared her head.

He stood and looked down his long muzzle at her for a moment. She let him speak. "Thank you for your help, Miss Stone. Er, and you can expect to receive an official letter of thanks from the department."

"I'm glad to have been of help." She waited. At the end of her police novels, if there had been a bright and helpful civilian, especially if she was a girl, one of the police usually tried to kiss her. So far, her experience had not quite played out like the novels; nobody at the end of one of her novels had to work out how to hold a household together.

The wolf shuffled back and forth, and his tail flicked to the side. He looked down in a way that was really rather endearing. "You're a very bright and attractive young lady…"

She took advantage of his hesitation to hold up a paw. "If I may, Sergeant?" He nodded. "I am…seeing someone. Not that I don't appreciate the sentiment."

His lips pulled back from a wide smile, long canine teeth showing. "Oh, I'm sorry if I gave the wrong impression. I was simply going to ask if I might call on you for help with a case now and again."

"A…police case?"

"Of course." He tapped his nose. "You have a good instinct for people, I think. Better than—well, let's just say another insight would be welcome."

The delicate difference in his scent was only just at the edge of her perception, but she thought she had been right about what he'd originally intended to ask. Still, he had handled it well, and she had to admit that she liked working with him. He'd thought quickly, improvised the trap for Mrs St. Clair, and had respected Ellie's opinions. "I'd be honoured to help," she said.

He extended a paw. "Until we meet again."

"Oh," she said, taking his large, strong fingers in hers, "as it happens, there is one more thing you might do for me, if you would be so kind…"

•

Ellie had been elected by the staff to make their case, since it was her idea to begin with. She found John St. Clair in his room, standing next to three closed suitcases of matching red leather, holding a letter in his paw. He put it down on his desk as she walked in. "Good morning, Ellie. Come to say good-bye?" His smile was wan, forced, and the morning light caught the edge of one black ear, leaving the rest of his face in shadow.

"I hope not, sir." She smiled. "We—all the staff of Tremontaine—we want to ask you to stay, to be Mr St. Clair of Tremontaine. It would mean a lot to us, and to your family."

More life came into his smile, just a touch. "It means a lot to hear that," he said. "Unfortunately, it is quite impossible."

"Sir, with respect, I don't believe—"

"I *know*, Ellie. I know better than anyone how quickly rumours spread." He clenched a fist. "How a boy at school can be called names by people he hasn't even *met*. How people take hearsay and…and innocent comments…and they make your life hell with it."

"Sir…"

"Let alone when they have actually got something to talk about! Those blasted police, nosing about in the room and then refusing to take my word for it…"

"It appeared to be an accident, sir."

"Yes, indeed." His smile was gone, his lips set in a thin line so that just the tips of his fangs showed. "That makes it all better, doesn't it? Just an accident. We'll just have them go back and pick up the box and this time do it right, and then there won't be any problem."

Ellie coughed delicately. "The box?"

John stared at her as though she were crazy. "You were there, Ellie, you know bloody well what box."

"Oh!" She perked up as though she'd only just realised what he was talking about. "You mean that box that Mr Trevayn put in your room to hide it?"

"Don't be ridiculous," he said, and then stopped. "What did you say?"

"Flora and I worked out the mistake," Ellie said. "Because Flora saw the box when she was doing the rooms, and Mr Trevayn had it. But after Mr St. Clair was shot, he must have known it would look bad for him to be caught with a gun box in his room. So he hid it in yours, and that's where the police found it."

It pleased her to see the young fox's jaw gape open. "Nobody would believe that," he choked out.

"So noble of you to try to safeguard your father's business partner's honour while this important business deal was going on. At great personal risk to yourself. Rest assured, Flora is making certain all the tradespeople know exactly what *truly* happened. I have made sure that Sergeant Cooke and the rest of the police understand it as well."

"Ellie," he said feebly.

She held up a paw. "I know it has been a trying week for you, sir. I'm sure you would agree you need peace and quiet, and what's more, your sister needs you, too. Imagine, she thought she was about to realise all her dreams, and then she found that Mr Trevayn lied to her and murdered her father. She'll need a shoulder to cry on."

"Nobody will believe the story." He turned his head, lowered it so that only the tip of his ear was lit by the sun.

"They will. Enough will. And the ones who don't?" Ellie waved a paw. "Let them talk. There's gossip to keep a town busy for a year, and the people who know you, they'll stand by you."

One ear flicked up. The gleam of his eyes shone from the shadow. "Like the staff?"

"Of course the staff will, sir." The sunlit ear flicked, but John stayed silent. Ellie thought of Miss Turner and went on. "And you might be surprised, sir, how welcoming people will be. After all, you're a kind person. You're no murderer. And when you share secrets with people, those are your family."

A flash of white showed in his muzzle. "I haven't much family remaining. I'd best take what's given me, eh?"

"We'd be very happy if you'd remain. Just for a week, at first, but we hope it'll be more permanent than that."

He stared down at the letter he'd dropped. Ellie turned to leave, but his voice stopped her. "Ellie."

"Sir?"

"Why not my sister? Why not just ask Mary to stay?"

Ellie considered. "Miss Mary might stay, but Tremontaine would become her dowry. And who knows whom she might marry? He might have no interest in the estate. Miss Mary may go off to Oxford."

John's lip twisted briefly at the mention of Oxford, but he nodded slowly, his slender muzzle dipping to the floor and coming up to rest his eyes on her again. "Is that the reason?"

"It just seems safer to have both of you living here."

"I see." And she thought he did, with his fox's cunning breaking through the self-pity, though he did not so much as glance up toward the room she shared with Abby. "Ellie, on my behalf, please extend heartfelt thanks to the staff. Tell them I have decided to remain here to ease my sister through her grief. Family comes first, after all. Then I will decide whether to return to America or not."

"Yes, sir."

He stopped her again as she was stepping out of his doorway. "Ellie, what was—what was Father paying you?"

She told him. He lifted a paw to rub his chin. "In my estimation, that seems a trifle low. I will have Mr Pearson see to it."

"Thank you, sir."

The fox smiled warmly. "Thank me in a week. I still doubt whether these things can be patched up so easily, but I admit I am being swayed by your confidence."

Ellie smiled and hurried upstairs to tell Abby the good news.

•

That evening, Ellie lay side-by-side with Abby, a blanket covering their fur against the chill in the air, their paws drifting lazily up and down the soft curves of the rabbit's hips, the weasel's breasts, the rabbit's shoulder, the weasel's slender arm. It was a joy just to be close to Abby this way, and for many long minutes, neither of them felt any need to speak.

Abby broke the silence. "You're quite clever, dear. Did you know?"

"I suspected." Ellie leaned over and kissed her lover's long ear. "But thank you. It was a difficult thing to get one's head around, but you know, once you worked out who was keeping secrets only about their private lives, there weren't many secrets left."

"And you convinced Mister John to stay."

"Maybe. For a little while."

"His bags were packed, and today Donald unpacked them."

"I think Donald will miss Mr St. Clair most, of all the staff," Ellie mused. "It will do him good to have a Mr St. Clair around. Otherwise he would certainly be let go."

"Donald would do well." Abby splayed her paw flat on Ellie's stomach and ruffled with her fingertips. "Dholes get all the best personal servant jobs with foxes and wolves. You'd be a good senior housekeeper."

"Me?" Ellie wriggled, and smiled. "I'd much rather rule a kitchen. But I'm just as happy working with Miss Turner."

"It's a good staff we've got, and no question." Abby sighed, her breath all green vegetables and love across Ellie's nose.

The door opened on this remark, and Flora stuck her whiskered head in. "Oh, sorry. Wrong door." She closed it behind her, pretending to shield her eyes as she moved through the room.

Ellie laughed. "It's a family, not a staff."

"Oh, well then." Flora lowered her paw and grinned at them. "Here's hoping things settle back to normal. Good job convincing Master John to stay, El. I suppose I will have to learn to call him Mr St. Clair properly, now. Didn't think you could do it, and I believe you could talk the horns off a ram. Well, not Mr Eldridge. But how you figured it all out…" She stopped and leaned against the bathroom door. "When you called the doctor because I drank the tea—were you really scared? Or was it all a ploy to make the missus talk?"

"No, I was scared," Ellie said. "Bitter tea and sleeping-powder and—I just didn't know." Under the covers, she squeezed Abby's paw. "I realised then, though, that even if Mrs St. Clair were completely justified in—in doing what she did, I would always be nervous."

The otter tapped the frame of the door. "Thank you, then. I like to think there's someone watching out for me." She coughed. "Even if I dose myself with sleeping-powder."

"Always."

"Good night, you two." She winked at them and then walked back through the bathroom to her room.

"Family," Abby said with an exasperated sigh.

"We must love them." Ellie slid her paw up Abby's chest and let it linger. "Can I ask you something, old soul?"

"You can do what you like while your paw's there."

"Do you feel better about us?"

The rabbit turned her head, one eye meeting Ellie's. "Right now?"

"In general."

"You mean, because you called the doctor because I drank a little bit of tea that you thought might have been poisoned?"

"I mean, because we've had Mrs St. Clair dressing in her husband's suits to meet a girl down in the village. And Miss Mary sneaking around with her father's business partner. And Mr Giles with his philandering, of course, and then that Japanese fox and…" She didn't want to mention Martin Trevayn in case Abby still had bad memories.

Indeed, the rabbit shuddered lightly, but did say, "That was faked, you said."

"People believed it, though. And of course, Mister John with his… well, his curiosities."

Abby laughed. "The poor boy was so embarrassed." She hesitated. "Maybe, if he stays…we can ask him where he got them."

Ellie raised an eyebrow. "Why, Miss White." Her paw drifted through fields of snowy white and rested in a certain spot. "Are you saying I'm not enough for you?"

"No-oo." The rabbit squirmed pleasurably. "I'm just saying, it might be interesting to, to maybe experiment a little. Broaden our…horizons."

If Abby were even considering talking to Mr St. Clair about his "curiosities," then it was a sign she felt better about their relationship and their position in the house. The warmth that suffused Ellie came not only from the rabbit next to her and the love they shared—she would ask Mister John herself, if Abby really wanted to try something new, but not now and probably not for many weeks—but from her pride in having kept the house together, having kept their home intact.

"What are you thinking of?" Abby murmured softly.

Ellie pressed up close to her, and her paw renewed its caresses. "Just the restaurant we're going to have."

"You in the kitchen."

"You as the hostess."

"Oh, El." Abby shuddered again, with pleasure this time. "It's going to be such a lovely place. Tell me again…how many tables we'll have."

About the Author

Kyell Gold began writing furry fiction a long, long time ago. In the early days of the 21st century, he got up the courage to write some gay furry romance, first publishing his story "The Prisoner's Release" in Sofawolf Press's adult magazine "Heat." He has since won twelve Ursa Major awards for his stories and novels, and his acclaimed novel "Out of Position" co-won the Rainbow Award for Best Gay Novel of 2009. His novel "Green Fairy" was nominated for inclusion in the ALA's "Over the Rainbow" list for 2012.

He was not born in California, but now considers it his home. He loves to travel and dine out with his husband Kit Silver, and can be seen at furry conventions around the world. More information about him and his books is available at *http://www.kyellgold.com*.

About the Artist

Sara Miles, formerly known as Sara Palmer, emerged onto the scene in the late 1990's under the fan name of "Caribou". A random web search for art supplies led her to an archive, and the rest was history. Priding herself on diversity, she enjoys working in traditional and digital media and has undertaken illustration, commission and comic work. She has been Guest of Honor to Anthrocon and Furfright, has won several Ursa Majors for her illustration work, and has hosted many panels at conventions over the years. Her current projects include co-owning Tigerdile.com, a specialty stream site, and Halfway Hotel, a comic project about Life in the Afterlife. She currently resides in a 230 year old house in rural New England and is owned by a family and many pets.

About the Publisher

FurPlanet publishes original works of furry fiction. You can explore their selection at *http://www.furplanet.com*.

What Are Cupcakes?

"Cupcakes" are short and sweet, standalone novellas that fill the gap between a short story and a novel. In 2009, a trio of furry writers were lamenting the lack of places to publish novellas they'd written. Kyell Gold, foozzzball, and Rikoshi had exchanged their works and helped each other refine them, and approached FurPlanet with the idea of creating a line of quality novellas by trusted writing names.

To date, the Cupcake novellas have won two Ursa Major awards and met with critical acclaim. "The Mysterious Affair of Giles" is the seventh in the line.